'It's a beautiful night,' she said softly, hoping for some response.

'Not especially,' he replied without looking at her.

A lump lodged in Jennifer's throat. 'Look, Clay,' she said, 'I realise that you got the impression that I let you down, but it wasn't . . .'

'Just drop it,' he said gruffly. 'I know what you were thinking.'

'You do not!' Jennifer cried, tears welling in her eyes.

'I said drop it!' Clay said, giving Jennifer an angry glance. 'I was a fool to expect anything except what happened.'

Clay had withdrawn from her so completely, he was so different from his previously warm, friendly self, that she could hardly tell he was the same person. When he said nothing more she said a quick goodnight and went back into her room. Once inside, she flung herself on her bed, buried her face in her pillows, and let out a scream of frustration. Why, oh why, if she wasn't going to go along with Clay, hadn't she just kept her mouth shut!

A MAN UNTAMED

BY

KATHERINE ARTHUR

MILLS & BOON LIMITED
ETON HOUSE   18-24 PARADISE ROAD
RICHMOND   SURREY   TW9 1SR

First published in Great Britain 1990
by Mills & Boon Limited

© Katherine Arthur 1990

Australian copyright 1990
Philippine copyright 1990
This edition 1990

ISBN 0 263 76673 X

Set in Times 11 on 11½ pt.
01 – 9005 – 54036

Typeset in Great Britain by JCL Graphics, Bristol

Made and Printed in Great Britain

NEVER MARRY A COWBOY

Never marry a cowboy
He'll break your heart in two.
He's a fighter, a loner,
A man you can't tame,
No matter what you do.

Barbara Eriksen

CHAPTER ONE

'I HEAR the helicopter!' The little blonde girl slammed her maths book shut and ran to the window. 'I see it. Uncle Clay's coming! Come and see, Jennifer. It's neat!'

'Coming, Pam.' Jennifer Tarkinton deposited a pile of plates on the kitchen counter and hurried to peer out of the window beside the little girl. A shiver of combined nerves and excitement went through her. At last she was going to meet Clayton Cooper, the man who had hired her to be the accountant for the huge Bar-C Ranch.

During the day she had received what seemed to be very conflicting reports on her new employer's disposition. Ten-year-old Pam, his ward, made him sound warm and loving. She obviously adored him, even though she said he might come in 'roaring like a tiger' from a day of battling against snow-drifts in search of starving cattle. The ranch foreman, Clarence Williams, portrayed him as a stern taskmaster. 'Very particular,' he called him, and likely to be 'fit to be tied' if losses to the blizzard were high. To Clarence's wife Nell, the housekeeper, Clayton Cooper was a perpetually tardy man who seldom arrived on time for dinner, yet expected to find it hot when he got there. So far, Jennifer was sure of only one thing: Clayton Cooper sounded nothing like the Hollywood version of a millionaire cattle baron, a man who either spent his time at a desk, manipulating huge sums of money, or rode about looking elegant on a glistening steed while others did the hard work of the ranch for him. For, according to Clarence, more than anything else Clayton Cooper loved 'cowboyin''.

A perimeter of lights came on, illuminating the flat area between the big house and Nell and Clarence Williams' small home. The helicopter hovered, then settled down. A tall man in a sheepskin jacket jumped out, his gold hair whipping in the propeller wash. He turned back and lifted something down in his arms, and then ran, stooped over, towards the door.

'He's got a calf!' Pam cried.

A calf? In the house? Jennifer stared as Nell, obviously accustomed to such events, muttered a soft, 'Oh, lord,' and then swung into action.

'Pam, get those old blankets. Cookie, thaw some colostrum out in the microwave. Jennifer, get the door. Now where'd I put that bottle?' She flung open a cupboard and pulled out a huge nursing bottle just as Jennifer flew by to open the door in the back entrance for Clayton Cooper, who was arriving home with a newborn calf in his arms.

A blast of cold air came through the opened door, followed by a current of warmth that Jennifer later realised was generated by nothing more than the electric excitement of Clay's overpowering personality.

'Heavy son of a gun,' Clayton Cooper said, staggering through the door with his huge, inert burden. 'Found him on the way back. His mama didn't make it. We've got to warm him up, fast.' He gave Jennifer a quick, penetrating glance. 'You're Jenny. I'm Clay. Grab some of those towels and start rubbing this fellow.' He indicated a shelf next to the washing-machine with a jerk of his head, and then lowered the calf on to the blankets that Pam had brought.

As if propelled by the diamond fire of his bright blue eyes, Jennifer rushed to do his bidding. So this, she thought breathlessly, as she grasped the stack of towels, was to be her introduction to her new employer. Never in her wildest dreams had she imagined it would be anything like this!

Only a few hours before, Jennifer had arrived at the airport in Bozeman, Montana, expecting to be met by Clayton Cooper. When he had not been inside the terminal, she had carried her bags outside and waited at the kerb, expecting any moment to see someone tall and handsome drive up in an expensive car and announce that he was Clayton Cooper, cattle baron, arriving to meet Ms Jennifer Tarkinton, accountant. Instead, she had been liberally splashed by a spray of slushy mist from the dirty, battered pick-up truck which had stopped in front of her.

A small, wiry man, leathery-faced, wearing a weather-beaten cowboy hat and a sheepskin jacket, jumped out of the truck.

'Sorry,' he growled, frowning as if he were more sorry that Jennifer had been in the way than he was for splashing her. He looked her up and down, his mouth in a grimace that indicated disapproval of everything from her sleek black topknot to her trim ankles above black, high-heeled pumps. 'You Ms Tarkinton?'

'Uh, yes, I am,' Jennifer answered almost reluctantly. 'Are you Mr Cooper?' If he was, this was certainly a let-down. Over the telephone, Clayton Cooper had sounded tall, broad-shouldered, and handsome—if a voice could sound that way.

The man gave a short negative jerk of his head. 'Just

one of the hands.' He pronounced just, 'jess'. 'The boss is of trying to feed cattle. Sorry I'm late. Almost forgot you were coming.' He picked up Jennifer's bags. 'Don't know why he had to hire someone from out of town, anyway,' she heard him mutter as he slung her bags unceremoniously into the back of the truck.

Jennifer was not sure why, either, but she had wanted desperately to get away from Chicago and had quickly answered the advertisement for the accounting job that Clayton Cooper had placed in a national newspaper. A ranch near Bozeman, Montana, had sounded like heaven, a haven of peace and beauty where she could escape both from her perennially quarrelsome parents and the shock of discovering that the man she had considered marrying had a sadistic streak she had never suspected.

'Get on into the truck,' the man said, heading for the driver's side without offering to open the door for Jennifer.

She nodded, and climbed into the truck cab, which was as unprepossessing as the exterior. There was a definite aura of cow country about it, mixed with a strong odour from an air freshener, shaped like a pair of cowboy boots, which hung from the rear-view mirror. The dashboard was dusty and littered with assorted tools, books of matches, and cigarette papers. There was no doubt that she was heading for a ranch, Jennifer thought, clasping her hands together in suppressed excitement. She might have imagined that even a cattle baron's pick-up trucks would be especially fancy, but this was the real thing, and she was about to head off towards the towering, snow-covered mountains with a man who was obviously a real cowboy.

'I didn't catch your name,' she said, when the man

got into the truck cab beside her.

'Guess I forgot to tell you,' he said. 'Clarence Williams.' He gave Jennifer another quick glance as he started the truck. 'Hope you've got some regular clothes with you. Don't have much need for high-heeled shoes where we're going.'

'Oh, I've got boots and walking shoes and jeans,' Jennifer said quickly, although she would never admit to this Clarence person that the cowboy boots were her first pair, and brand-new. 'I just wanted to make a good first impression on Mr Cooper.'

'Mmmph,' said Clarence, and then fell silent. He flipped on the radio, which came on with a blast of country and western music. 'Never marry a cowboy,' wailed a female vocalist. 'He'll break your heart in two . . .'

So much for the first impression she'd made on Clarence, Jennifer thought with a sigh. She could see by the thick gold ring on his leathery hand that someone had married that cowboy. Somehow, Clarence didn't look like much of a heartbreaker. Hard to get along with, maybe. Oh, well, she didn't have to please him. Only Clayton Cooper.

Outside, the spectacular scenery more than made up for Clarence's lack of enthusiasm. They turned south off the main highway, along roads recently ploughed, with snow banks piled on either side. Huge, snow-laden pines flanked the road. Now and then, a gust of wind whipped a shimmering, iridescent shower from the branches. It looked, Jennifer thought, like a perfect Christmas card winter-wonderland scene, but she doubted that the ranchers who had to battle the drifts to save their hungry cattle found it so enchanting. A killer blizzard, the news reports had described the freakish spring storm which had struck the Rocky Mountains and the western great plains three days ago.

She looked over at Clarence, who was staring straight ahead and driving with one hand while he rolled a cigarette with the other. 'Will the snow last long this time of year?' she asked.

Clarence did not stop his cigarette making. He calmly licked the paper, and then sealed it, then put it in his mouth.

'How long——?' Jennifer began more loudly, thinking that perhaps he had not heard her over the blaring radio. She stopped as he gave her a withering glance.

'I heard ya,' he said. He lit his cigarette, and then said, 'Till it melts.'

Jennifer frowned. 'I knew that,' she said sharply. Was Clarence being disagreeable, or did he think she was an idiot? 'What I meant was——'

'I know whatcha meant,' Clarence said grimly. 'Lady, if I knew how long it'd be before the snow melts, then I'd know how long we're going to have to try and feed the cows that got caught where they can't get any feed or whether we should try to bust a trail and get 'em out before it snows again. I oughta be out there helping the boss. He's sure gonna be fit to be tied if we already lost a bunch of calves.' After that lengthy speech, Clarence fell silent, puffing on his cigarette, his attention riveted on the snowy road that now turned in a series of switchbacks and climbed ever higher.

It was obvious to Jennifer that Clarence was not happy at having drawn the assignment of picking her up. It was also apparent from what he had said that Clayton Cooper had a bad temper. Of course, no rancher would be happy at losing part of his calf crop. But 'fit to be tied'? Jennifer shivered a little nervously. She hoped she wouldn't have to meet her new employer while he was in that state.

She stared out of the window and chewed on her lip, trying to keep calm and appreciate the scenery rather than let her active imagination conjure a fiercely scowling Clayton Cooper, instead of the friendly, smiling man she had hoped to meet. She had had more than enough of bickering, quarrelsome people. All of her life, she had watched her parents fight. Her mother would scream and throw things, her father would slam out of the door, vowing never to come back. Even when Jennifer had moved to her own apartment she could not escape. After an argument, one or the other of her parents would appear at her door, eager to tell his or her version of the truth. The last straw had been when her mother had started nagging at her to marry Alan Bailey, head of the accounting firm for which Jennifer had worked. Her father had argued against it, for no apparent reason. Soon they had been shouting at each other, leaving Jennifer to watch unhappily, as if she had no part at all in the decision.

'Stop it!' Jennifer had finally yelled, loudly enough to be heard. When they had finally stopped and looked at her, she had burst into tears of sheer frustration. 'I've had enough of listening to you two fight,' she sobbed. 'I'm not going to marry Alan Bailey, and I'm not going to stay around here any longer. I'm going to find a job somewhere far away!'

Jennifer had not had a chance to tell her parents her reason for rejecting Alan's proposal, but as she had driven back to her apartment that night she had thought grimly that it was just as well that she didn't. It would probably have precipitated an even worse scene.

Ordinarily, Alan was charming and sophisticated company, if a little dull and humourless. But the previous night he had had more to drink than usual. When she had asked him, quite calmly, to stop trying to put his hand inside her blouse, he had shaken her violently and slapped her so hard that her eye had swelled shut, all the while cursing her in words she would never care to repeat. In the morning, he had been very apologetic, but just the sight of him had made Jennifer feel sick. She had given him notice that she was leaving Bailey and Scruggs, and on her lunch-hour had picked up several newspapers to search for a new job. At first she had thought only of another job in Chicago. Then her eye had fallen on the advertisement in a national business newspaper: 'Experienced accountant needed for large Montana cattle ranch. Send résumé to Box 13, c/o this newspaper.'

The more she had thought about it, the more Jennifer had thought that job might be just the thing. Listening to her parents fight had convinced her. She had sent off her résumé, and in only a few days Clayton Cooper had called and offered her the job.

For a change, Jennifer's parents had joined forces, trying to persuade her not to go so far away to 'that wilderness'. Her mother had been sure she was making a terrible mistake, passing up the chance to marry Alan Bailey. 'You're almost twenty-eight, and you're not going to have that many more good opportunities,' she'd said.

'Maybe so,' Jennifer had replied, 'but I'm going.'

Alan, unable to believe that Jennifer was rejecting him over 'that one little episode', had predicted that she would return before the summer was over. 'You're not used to being around such crude people,' he'd said in his arrogant, superior way.

Jennifer had looked at him contemptuously and walked away. He was a fine one to call others crude.

Crude? Jennifer cast a quick glance at Clarence's craggy, weather beaten profile. He would be recognised as a cowboy anywhere. He might be more rough-hewn than Alan, but at least he didn't look as if he would shrink from anything that meant getting his fingernails dirty. His grouchiness aside, he looked strong and reliable, the kind of man who could be counted on to tackle a tough job and see it through.

The scenery was growing ever more spectacular, too. No wilderness, it looked like a place that God had blessed on a grand scale. They were now skirting a mountainside in a series of curves that had begun to descend again. Below them was a creek, its icy waters bubbling across large rocks. Gradually, they approached the level of the creek, then, quite abruptly it seemed, they rounded a final bend and came out of the canyon into a wide valley. In the distance, mountains cut a jagged swath of white across the most brilliantly blue sky Jennifer had ever seen. She let out an inadvertent gasp and Clarence glanced at her sharply.

'This is so beautiful,' she said, giving him a quick smile. 'Everything looks so clean and fresh. The air is so clear. With the mountains all around it looks almost unreal. Like a movie set. Is this where the ranch is?'

'Yep,' Clarence replied laconically.

The main road followed the edge of the valley, but Clarence turned off on to a narrower road which followed the stream down the centre of the valley. 'Gotta send Porky out to plough some more. This ain't gonna do,' he grumbled. 'Have to back up ten miles if we met someone down a piece. That lazy so-and-so never does his share.' He jerked his thumb to the right.

There was nothing to be seen but a gate between two tall fence posts which supported a crossbar bearing a small sign with the Bar-C Ranch brand, a large C crossed by a horizontal bar. Behind the fence, a neatly ploughed narrow road led off through an expanse of white snow in the direction Clarence had indicated.

'I though we were going to the Bar-C Ranch,' Jennifer said, frowning. 'Isn't that it?'

'It's all part of the ranch,' Clarence replied, giving Jennifer a look that plainly indicated he thought her question was stupid. 'This whole valley's Bar-C. Part of the mountains, too.'

'Oh, I see,' Jennifer said, although she still wasn't sure about his complaint. 'Does another rancher live back there, who's supposed to help keep this road clear?'

'The boss's brother, Forrest,' Clarence said, his gravelly voice indicating dislike. 'He lives in the old family ranch house, along with his father and a nurse and a housekeeper. Matt Cooper's an ornery old cuss, but he's a good man. If he wasn't sick in bed I don't think he could stand living with that stuffed-shirt son of his. He ain't nothin' like the boss. Forrest don't like to get his hands dirty if he can help it.'

'I've known men like that,' Jennifer said when Clarence paused, 'but I can't imagine someone like that on a ranch. Doesn't he do anything with the cattle?'

Clarence snorted. 'He's supposed to be in charge of marketing the cattle, but I don't think he's doing much of a job. Too busy chasing the women. That's why his wife left him.'

The roof of a large house was now visible beyond a slight rise in the ground, smoke curling up from the chimney. There, Jennifer thought, lived Forrest Cooper, who sounded entirely too much like Alan Bailey. Alan was too tight with his money to be much of a womaniser, but she wondered, with his other hidden flaw, just how loyal a husband he would have been. It occurred to Jennifer that she really knew very little about Clayton Cooper, either.

'Thirty-five, and I've got all of my own teeth,' he had answered with a laugh when she had asked him to tell her a little about himself. 'Not all former champion bronco riders can say that.' He hadn't mentioned a wife. She hoped he didn't share his brother's attitude towards women.

'Is—uh—Mr Clayton Cooper married?' Jennifer asked, hoping that Clarence would not misinterpret her question as meaning that she was hunting for a husband.

'You mean you don't know?' Clarence queried back, giving Jennifer a surprised stare.

'Well, no. No, I don't,' Jennifer replied. 'He didn't tell me and I didn't think it would be polite to ask.'

'I'll be darned,' Clarence said, smiling suddenly. 'I guess I never will understand this women's lib.'

'Do you mean to tell me,' Jennifer demanded, having interpreted Clarence's oblique statements as meaning that Clayton Cooper was not married, and her motives were already suspect, 'that you thought I came here to try and catch a husband?'

'It occurred to me,' Clarence replied, giving Jennifer a sideways look. 'There's a lot of ladies that would like to have the boss get interested in them, but he doesn't have the time. This is a mighty big outfit to run with as little help as he gets from his brother. The old man used to help, until he got sick. Now it's most all up to the boss.'

'He must be a very hard-working man,' Jennifer said, relieved at Clarence's statement, which also helped to explain his initial reaction to her. 'I'm here to work, too, and that's all. I just wanted to get away from the city.'

'That's good,' Clarence said, although Jennifer thought he still looked a little sceptical. 'The boss needs all the help he can get on that accounting business. He doesn't like that part of ranching at all. Doesn't like sittin' around.'

'Then he goes out and works all of the time like he is today? I thought he'd have cowhands to do most of that for him,' Jennifer said, surprised.

'The boss always says you can't make any money if you pay people to do your work for you. We've got a lot of cowhands, but the boss is always right there, whether it's working cattle or fixing fences, 'cause that's what he likes to do. He says when he has to quit the cowboyin' part he'll get out of ranching. He's always been that way.

'You've known him for a long time, then?'

'Yep. Since he was a baby. I've worked for the Bar-C since I was eighteen. Now I'm sixty.' He sighed. 'Not many young cowboys left, 'cept in the rodeos. And they ain't real cowboys. Put one of them show-offs in a real round-up and they'd be tuckered out in a day.' He gave Jennifer another quick look. 'You a good rider?' he asked.

Jennifer shook her head. 'No rider at all. The only thing I'm really good with is numbers.'

Clarence smiled smugly. 'The boss'll have you on a horse in no time. Soon as the snow melts, I'd bet. Well, here we are. The *real* Bar-C ranch house.'

While Jennifer tried to suppress her consternation at the idea that Clayton Cooper might require her to ride

a horse, Clarence turned the truck between another set
of the tall gateposts crowned by the Bar-C brand. They
crossed the creek they had followed, the ranch road now
meandering alongside a smaller creek towards a stand
of pines which towered over a spread of low buildings.
When they drew nearer, Jennifer saw that some of the
buildings were, in fact, quite large barns, surrounded by
high pens made of sturdy wood. In a few of the pens,
which had been sheltered from the drifting snow by the
barns, some large, long-legged cattle were munching on
piles of hay.

'Just got in some new breeding stock before the storm
hit,' Clarence said. 'Adding some Chianina blood to the
mix.'

'I've heard that's a good idea,' Jennifer said, trying
to sound knowledgeable. She had read everything she
could find about cattle once she'd decided to take the
job with Clayton Cooper, but still was not sure she could
tell one kind of cow from another.

'Time'll tell,' Clarence said philosophically. He
stopped in front of a long building with several doors,
which looked very much like a small motel. Parked in
front of the building was a huge tractor with a
snow-plough blade on the front of it. 'Jess be a minute,'
Clarence said as he got out. 'Gotta tell Porky to fix that
plough job up right so cars can pass a few places. The
boss don't like things done halfway.'

While Jennifer watched, Clarence knocked on one of
the doors and spoke briefly to the younger man who
answered. The younger man nodded, smiling agreeably,
as if he did not in the least mind being told he should do
the job better.

'Porky's new,' Clarence said, as he climbed back into
the truck. 'He don't know how particular the boss is.'

'Are you the foreman?' Jennifer asked, trying not to think about how her work might please the particular Clayton Cooper.

'Yep,' Clarence replied. The road swung past another barn. 'Horse barn,' he said. They came to a long row of pines which made a ninety-degree turn in front of them. 'The boss's grandma planted these pines for a windbreak. They had their first little house here.' They made the turn, went past the end of the pines, then angled back behind them on a drive which curved in front of a sprawling log house with a two-storey centre section and one-storey wings on either side. An overhanging roof, a balcony on the second storey and a low porch on the first gave the house a Swiss-chalet appearance in the midst of the snow.

'What a beautiful house!' Jennifer exclaimed.

'The boss likes nice things,' Clarence said, proceeding around the house towards the back. 'I expect I ought to take you in the front door, but the back's easier. Shovelled off the back porch myself.' He brought the truck to a stop. 'Guess you're stayin' right here,' he said. 'Me and Nell live over there.' He pointed to a smaller house, a short distance away across a level area from which the snow had been removed. 'Nell's my wife. Forty years now. She's the cook and housekeeper. Head honcho in here . . .' he indicated the big house '. . . but not over there.' He grinned and pointed to his home.

'That's the way it usually is,' Jennifer said, thinking that Clarence must be a pretty good head honcho in his own domains if he had been with the Coopers for over forty years. She got out of the truck, and started up the small path that led to the back porch. Before she could mount the stairs, the door flew open.

'Good lord, Clarence, I thought you'd never get

back,' said the rotund woman who opened the door. 'Mr Cooper's having a fit because he can't get hold of Mike Garland. He wants him to bring the helicopter and pick him up at the north-east camp. His horse went lame and he had to walk out of Fox Canyon. He says Mike should be through dropping hay by now, but I can't find him. I've tried and tried to get him on the two-way.'

'I'll find him,' Clarence said, depositing Jennifer's bags inside the door. 'This here's Ms Tarkinton.' So saying, he gave his wife a peck on the cheek and hurried off again.

'You tell Mike to tell Clay to get back here before his dinner gets cold,' she called after her departing husband. She turned and smiled conspiratorially at Jennifer. 'That man's never on time. He knows I'll keep his dinner hot, but there's no point letting him think I don't expect him to get here,' she said. She looked Jennifer up and down. 'Mighty pretty city girl.' She bent and peered into Jennifer's eyes. 'Green eyes. Hmmph. Black hair and green eyes. Different. Most everyone around here has blonde hair and blue eyes, or grey hair like me. Or no hair, like Clarence. You ever been on a ranch before?'

'No, I haven't,' Jennifer replied. 'It's all going to be new to me. But I do have some ranch clothes,' she added, thinking that perhaps Nell was as worried about that as Clarence had been.

Nell nodded. 'Well, you're young. I expect you'll get used to ranch life in a hurry. Didn't know much about it myself when I met Clarence. Now, let me get some help and I'll show you your room so you can get into some regular clothes. Come along.'

Nell bustled off, leading Jennifer through a swinging door from the tiled back entrance, which in reality was a large utility-room and pantry, two shelf-lined walls loaded with canned goods and cleaning supplies, the others containing a washer and drier and a huge freezer. They came into a big country kitchen, with an eating area at the far end so large that Jennifer could count twelve chairs around the oval pine table.

'Cookie, you grab Mrs Tarkinton's big suitcases,' Nell said to a tall young man who was busily peeling potatoes at the sink. 'Pam, you can bring the little bag. This here's the lady that's come to keep Mr Cooper's accounts.'

Cookie put down his potato, wiped his hands, and smiled. 'How do, Ms Tarkinton?' he said.

A little girl with curly blonde hair was seated at the table, working on what looked to Jennifer like schoolwork. 'Sure thing,' she said, slamming her book shut.

'Homework?' Jennifer asked her.

'Yeah,' the little girl named Pam answered. 'The school bus couldn't get through for two days, but they make us catch up anyway.' She ran after Cookie and picked up Jennifer's bag.

'Cookie here's my chief helper,' Nell said, as she led the group through a wide doorway towards the stairs which curved upwards to a balcony overlooking the two-storey living-room. 'Between us we do most of the cooking and cleaning. Pam's our little pet. Kind of ornery, but we like her anyway. She's Mr Cooper's ward. I think she'll be glad to have another female in the house. Gets kind of lonely for her sometimes, since Mr Cooper won't let her bring her horse in the house.'

Pam giggled. 'I tried to bring a pony in once when I was real little,' she explained. 'I was trying to get him upstairs when Uncle Clay caught me.'

'I'll bet that got him upset,' Jennifer said, imagining

what the meticulous Clayton Cooper would think of such a prank.

'Nah, he just laughed and laughed,' Pam said.

That, Jennifer thought, was the first encouraging thing she'd heard about Clayton Cooper's disposition. At least he was good-natured about a childish prank. At the top of the stairs, she glanced back at the huge living-room, and had a quick impression of bright colours, the warm glow of polished pine, and the sullen stare of an immense moosehead mounted on the stone fireplace chimney. She followed Nell down a central hall which divided the second storey and ended with a window overlooking the balcony on the front of the house. Nell went in through the last door on the right.

'This'll be your room,' she said. 'We already put that box of books you sent on over there,' she pointed, 'and the wardrobe's over there, the bath's there, and when the weather gets good you can go out that door on to the balcony. There's a fine view of the valley from there. Now, we'll clear out and let you get settled. Dinner's at six, but you can come down any time you're ready and get acquainted. There'll be six of the hands here for dinner, and we can always use some extra help.

'And I can use some help on my maths,' Pam said, hanging behind in the doorway. 'I'll bet you're good at that.'

'Pretty good,' Jennifer agreed. She could see that the little girl was reluctant to leave. 'Why don't you help me unpack, and then I can help you later?'

'OK,' Pam said. She looked questioningly at Nell. 'May I?'

'All right, but don't be a pest,' Nell said, ruffling Pam's curls.

Pam smiled happily and came back into Jennifer's

room. 'It's gonna be neat having you here,' she said, 'and I'm glad you're gonna help with my maths. Uncle Clay's probably going to be cross, if everything's gone wrong today. Besides, he's not very good at maths.'

While Pam chattered on about her horse, the ranch and her school, Jennifer opened her suitcases and began hanging things in the generous cedar-lined wardrobe. There was a huge dresser, with more drawer space than she had ever had in her own small apartment. The bed, a comfortable-looking four-poster, was covered in a wedding-ring-patterned handmade quilt, the bright colours echoed in the braided rug that set off a sitting area near the balcony windows, where there was a comfortable lounge chair, an antique rocker, a small desk, and a television set. It was a lovely room, but somehow Jennifer felt a little uncomfortable. She had imagined something more austere, perhaps set off by itself instead of right in with the family. Still, room and board had been part of her arrangement, and the room was plenty large enough for her to steal away and be alone when she wanted to.

She sent Pam into the large combination bath-and-dressing-room with her cases of cosmetics and toiletries, and then to the wardrobe with her shoes and boots.

'It doesn't look like you've used these boots,' Pam commented.

'They're new,' Jennifer said. 'I haven't had any use for boots where I've been working.'

'Well, you will now,' Pam said. 'We'll go riding together as soon as the snow melts.'

'I'm afraid I don't ride,' Jennifer said. 'The only time I tried it, when I was about your age, I fell and broke my arm.' She did not add the embarrassing fact that she had fallen from a pony harnessed in a pony ring at the fair.

Pam stared at her in disbelief. 'You don't ride? You can't live here and not ride!'

Jennifer smiled weakly. 'Well, maybe some day I'll get up my nerve and try it again. But I was hired to keep the books, not ride the horses.'

'You've gotta learn,' Pam said firmly. 'Just like I've gotta learn maths. You'd better put those boots on right now and get them broken in. Put on some jeans, too. Otherwise Uncle Clay's gonna think he hired someone who doesn't know anything about a ranch.'

'I never told him that I did, except for the business part,' Jennifer said with an amused smile. Pam was just as plain-spoken as Clarence and Nell. 'But I guess I'd better try to look right, hadn't I?' She had already noticed that even the heavy-set Nell was wearing jeans and a plaid flannel shirt beneath her apron. She picked out some jeans and a bright red turtle-neck sweater and retreated to the bathroom. A few minutes later she returned to the bedroom. 'Is this better?' she asked.

'Lots,' Pam said approvingly. She brought out Jennifer's boots, and Jennifer sat down and pulled them on, wondering if she was only asking for trouble in looking as if she was about to go riding. She had no intention of letting either Pam or Clayton Cooper browbeat her into doing so if she didn't want to, and she seriously doubted she was going to want to any time soon. 'Now, you look like a real cowgirl,' Pam said, when Jennifer stood up. 'Come on. I'll show you the rest of the house. Uncle Clay always does that when people come to visit.'

She went out of the door and crossed the hall. 'This is Uncle Clay's room,' she said, opening the door. 'It's just like yours, only he's kind of messy, and he only lets Nell clean it up once a week because he says he loses stuff if she does it every day.'

Jennifer quickly peeped in the door. The bed was unmade, and there were various articles of clothing draped over the furniture, several pairs of boots sitting near the bed. Rather surprising, she thought, for a man who was so 'particular'. But with the problems the blizzard had brought, he probably hadn't had time to pick up.

Next, Pam showed her two smaller bedrooms that were used for guests. 'Lots of other ranchers come and visit, and business people Uncle Clay knows,' she said, 'and sometimes Tanya stays over. She's Uncle Clay's brother's wife, but they don't live together any more. Sometimes she helps with the book-keeping.' She made a face and lowered her voice confidentially. 'I don't think she's very good at it, but I think Uncle Clay feels sorry for her and he's kind of soft-hearted. That's why I'm here.' She looked up at Jennifer. 'He's not really my uncle, but I call him that. See, my dad and mom were killed in a blizzard, trying to save some calves, when I was only five. I'm ten now. My dad worked for Uncle Clay, so he decided he'd keep me because he felt so bad about that and he liked me such a lot, and I liked him, too.'

'That was a good solution for both of you, then, wasn't it?' Jennifer said, bemused by this new revelation. Nothing anyone else had said would have led her to believe that Clayton Cooper was soft-hearted. But then, a lot of very tough people were soft touches for children and dogs.

Pam showed Jennifer her own room, the walls covered with rodeo posters and pictures of horses. 'I'm

gonna be a real cowgirl and ride in the rodeos,' she said.
'I'm already good at barrel racing.' Then she led the way
downstairs to the single-storey wings. 'This is Uncle
Clay's special room,' she said, taking Jennifer into a
large room with wood-panelled walls, soft red leather
chairs and a sofa, and, surprisingly, a grand piano. 'He
comes in here and reads and plays the piano,' Pam
added, answering the question that had entered
Jennifer's mind about who the musician might be. 'He's
teaching me to play.' She turned and went back to the
front entrance hall. 'That's the office,' she said, pointing
to the room opposite the 'special' room. 'I expect that's
where you'll be working, 'cause that's where Mr
McDonald worked before he quit. I'd show you, but it's
always locked when Uncle Clay's gone. He doesn't
want anyone messing around in there.'

'He'll probably show me later,' Jennifer said. 'Thank
you for the tour. This is a really beautiful house. I think
I'm going to like it here.'

'It's pretty nice, but I like the stables better,' Pam said.
She paused and looked up at Jennifer. 'Ms Tarkinton ...
can I call you something else? That makes you sound
too much like a schoolteacher. I want you to be my
friend.'

'Call me Jennifer,' Jennifer said quickly. 'I'd like to
be your friend, too.'

'Jennifer. That's a pretty name. Come on, we'd better
go and help Nell and Cookie with the dinner. There's a
lot of other people you've got to meet, too. And maybe
Uncle Clay will be back soon.' She grinned. 'But we
kind of hope he won't be back until after everyone else
is through eating, because he might come roaring in like
a tiger. He does that sometimes, but don't pay any
attention if he does. He's not really mean.'

'That's good to hear,' Jennifer said. Now, if she only knew which version of Clayton Cooper's temperament to believe, she could brace herself to face him. Like Pam, she felt she would as soon wait until after dinner to do so.

The dinner-hour passed swiftly, with still no sign of Clayton Cooper, although Clarence reported he had made contact with the helicopter pilot and sent him off to retrieve 'the boss' a couple of hours before. Jennifer had little time to brood about his impending arrival, for she had to try to learn the names of six more men, a friendly but rather taciturn group who mostly said, 'How do?' and then quickly cleaned up their dinners and returned to their own quarters. After that, she began to simultaneously help clear the table and give Pam some suggestions on her homework, thinking that so far the day had not turned out at all like she had expected, and totally unprepared for the new twist it was about to take.

The urgency of Clayton Cooper's attention to the calf seemed to spread to everyone in the room. In a matter of moments, Jennifer had grabbed the pile of towels and dropped to her knees beside the calf, flung an opened towel across its cold, motionless body and begun rubbing it vigorously around the head and shoulders.

'Colostrum's coming,' Nell said.

'Good.' Clay tossed off his coat, then knelt down and began rubbing the back end of the calf with another towel.

Cookie brought a portable electric heater and turned it on. Jennifer quickly began to perspire in her warm sweater, but she kept up her vigorous rubbing. Beside her, Clay worked on silently, intensely concentrated on what he was doing. He seemed to Jennifer, who glanced at him from time to time, to be lost in another world where he battled alone for the life of the calf. As a towel became damp, she flung it aside and took another, willing her aching arms to keep on rubbing as long as Clay kept working. Before long, the calf's soft coat was dry and it began to shiver.

'Good sign,' Clay said, giving Jennifer a nod and a wink of encouragement as she glanced at him again. He pushed back the lock of damp, gold hair which clung to his sweating forehead and then went back to work.

Good lord, but he's handsome, Jennifer thought. Even with his face streaked with sweat and smudges. She kept on rubbing, feeling as if she were in a trance, where the pain in her arms belonged to someone else and only the life of the little calf mattered. Soon its spasms of trembling came less often. Its tongue was no longer protruding, cold and lifeless, its wide, long-lashed eyes were no longer rolling fearfully.

'I think we're getting there,' Clay said. 'Stick your thumb in his mouth and see if he'll suck.'

Jennifer glanced at her new boss and quickly did as he instructed, thinking as she did so that there was something so compelling in his glance that it made a person stop thinking their own thoughts and do what he said without question. She nodded as the rough tongue curled around her thumb. 'He is,' she said.

'Good. Let's get him to his feet.' Clay stood up and lifted the calf's mid-section. The calf's wobbly legs splayed out in all directions, but Pam dropped to her knees and helped it get its hind legs in balance, while Jennifer propped up the front half. Nell came with the bottle and held the calf's head higher, dropping a little of the warm liquid on to its tongue, and then inserting the huge nipple into its mouth. It made a few slurping noises and then got a firm hold on the nipple and drank vigorously. 'Ya-hoo,' said Clayton Cooper, in a very subdued version of a cowboy yell. 'We've got us a real winner here. Sure am glad I spotted the little fellow.' He grinned down at Jennifer. 'Hey, Jenny, I thought you'd never been around cattle before. You're doing great.'

Jennifer could only stare at him and smile back, dazzled by the warmth of his smile. He seemed to exude a vitality that filled the little room, sweeping everything up in its magnetic field. Perhaps, she thought, even setting off a spark in the calf who had responded so well to their ministrations.

Clarence and two of the hands appeared at the door and exclaimed over the calf's excellent appearance. 'We've got the nursery pen all ready,' said Clarence. 'Clean straw and heat lamps. Ken and Flint'll take turns feeding the little guy until we find a momma that'll take him.'

'Good.' Clay nodded approvingly. ' Wrap him up and take him away. Now that he's got that colostrum in him, he should do fine.'

After the hands had carefully picked up the calf, Clay held his hand down to Jennifer. She grasped it unquestioningly and suddenly found herself in a bone-crushing hug that made her feel breathless and dizzy.

'Great work, Jenny,' he said again. He released her and laughed 'I'll bet this wasn't the kind of welcome you expected at the Bar-C.'

'No—no, not quite,' she replied, even in her confusion noticing how open and boyish his smile was. 'But it's been exciting.'

'That's the right idea,' Clay said approvingly. 'Life is an adventure. Enjoy it.' He turned up the sleeves of his plaid wool shirt and then went to the large laundry sink and turned on the tap. He lathered his hands and then bent to wash his face. As he splashed the water, he turned his head sideways to look at Jennifer. 'You know how that works? The colostrum?' he asked. When Jennifer shook her head, he went on, now drying his hands and face with a towel, 'It's the mother's first milk. Gives the calf the immunities it needs to survive. If they don't get it in the first few hours, it's no use trying to save them.'

'I see,' Jennifer said, nodding. She had the strange feeling that she had entered another world, the world of Clayton Cooper, the moment he came through the door. She watched and listened as he went back to giving out orders.

'Clarence, you stay while I eat and I'll give you a run-down on what happened this afternoon,' he said. 'Pam, you come here and give me a big hug and a kiss, and then see if Jenny minds reading you your bedtime story tonight, so I can get Clarence straightened out and then talk to her afterwards. Did you get your homework done?'

'Almost,' Pam said, clinging around Clay's neck and hugging him tightly as he bent towards her. 'Jenny's helping me with my maths.'

'That's great,' he said, lifting the little girl into his arms and holding her close for a moment before he put her down. 'I think Jenny's going to be more help around here than six cowboys.' He smiled over Pam's head at Jennifer. 'Hope you don't mind being called on again. Life isn't usually quite this hectic around here.'

'Oh, no,' Jennifer said quickly. 'I don't mind at all.' What Clay would say if she said she did mind she couldn't imagine. She doubted such a thought ever occurred to him He might look nothing like the standard Hollywood cattle baron, but the air of authority was unmistakable. 'Come on, Pam, let's get that maths finished,' she said, assuming the authority that had been given to her.

'Off you go,' Clay said, giving Pam a quick goodnight kiss. 'Jenny, I'll be ready to talk to you in about half an hour. Come on back down and we'll have some coffee.'

Restraining an impulse to say, 'Yes, sir,' and salute, Jennifer nodded. 'I will,' she said.

'How do you like Uncle Clay?' Pam asked with her usual directness, as Jennifer accompanied her up the stairs. 'He's . . . quite a man,' Jennifer answered, thinking as she did so that that was probably one of her grosser understatements. 'I can imagine him roaring like a tiger, the way you said he might, but he didn't seem very fierce tonight.'

'That's 'cause he found the calf and helped it,' Pam said with a knowing nod. 'That makes him happy. If he hadn't, he'd have been fierce, believe me. He loves all his cows so much that he can't stand to have any of them get hurt.'

'All ten thousand of them?' Jennifer asked sceptically.

'Every one,' said Pam. 'That's just the way he is.' She grinned at Jennifer. 'It was good you helped, so now he doesn't think you're some dumb city person who can't do anything.'

'I guess you're right about that,' Jennifer said with a sigh. Unfortunately, a dumb city person was exactly what she was, and Clayton Cooper was bound to find that out before long. She helped Pam tidy up the last of her maths problems. Then, when the little girl had put on her pyjamas, she read her a chapter from a book which, Pam informed her, was about a young girl who tamed a wild horse and became a champion rider, 'Like I'm going to be.'

When Jennifer had finished the chapter, Pam sat up and gave her a hug. 'I'm sure glad you decided to come here,' she said. 'I know Uncle Clay's glad, too. When he saw your picture that you sent, he didn't even look at any of the other applications. He said he'd hire you even if you couldn't add or subtract.'

Jennifer stared at Pam, feeling a sudden constriction in her throat. 'He did? I mean, he certainly didn't really mean that. He couldn't afford to hire someone who couldn't do the job right. Besides, Clarence said he's very particular.'

'I know,' Pam said with a grin. 'I think he just meant that you're pretty, and you're even prettier than your picture. But he's not fussy like Clarence says, either. It's kind of funny.' She paused and cocked her head thoughtfully, then shrugged. 'You'll see, when you get to know him,' she said cryptically.

'I suppose I will,' Jennifer said, although at the moment she was not sure whether she was prepared to get to know Clayton Cooper, who was obviously a man of many conflicting dimensions. She said goodnight to Pam, and then went to her room to tidy up her hair before going downstairs for her first professional meeting with her rather overwhelming 'boss'. It did not help at all to know about the remark he had made when he'd seen her picture. Clarence had implied he had little time for women, but apparently that didn't mean his interest was lagging. It made her feel unusually self-conscious.

Jennifer splashed her face with cold water, patted it dry, then tucked in the combs that held her hair in a neat topknot. 'I guess that will have to do,' she said, taking a deep breath and making a wry face at herself in the mirror. She straightened her shoulders. 'Forward, march,' she murmured, and resolutely went back downstairs to her appointed meeting. As she approached the door to the dining end of the country kitchen she heard Clayton Cooper laugh heartily.

'Clarence,' he said, 'stop clucking like an old hen. There's plenty of manpower down at that end to do the job.' At the sound of Jennifer's approaching footsteps he turned his head. 'Here's Jenny now. Come on in and sit down. Clarence tells me I'm getting soft just because I'm going to take tomorrow off to get you settled in and show you around the ranch. It seems to me it's the least I can do when such a pretty girl comes clear out here in the wilderness to keep my books for me.' He smiled, and Jennifer once again had the disconcerting sensation of an electric current that reached across the space between them.

She could think of nothing to say, so she smiled back and took the chair that Clay pulled out for her. She tried to include Clarence in her smile, but he avoided her eyes and stood up just as she sat down.

'Y'do want me to try and come up with a count on the losses tomorrow, don't you?' he asked. The raspy edge to his voice told Jennifer that he was irritated by something, probably something to do with her. She watched as Clay turned his attention back to Clarence, his smile fading instantly, replaced by a look of almost tragic sorrow.

'Yes, but I don't want to hear it, at least not until the snow melts,' he replied. 'It's going to be too damned depressing.'

He did really care, just as Pam had said, Jennifer

thought. He did not look like a man who was losing money, but rather like one who contemplated the loss of a dear friend.

Clarence pursed his mouth. 'Yessir,' he replied. He picked up his hat and coat from a chair and put them on. 'Goodnight,' he said with a nod to Clay. At last he acknowledged Jennifer's presence with another little nod. 'Goodnight , Ms Tarkinton.'

'Goodnight, Mr Williams,' she said, watching as he went out through the kitchen, giving a curt 'Goodnight' to Cookie, who was kneading vigorously at a mound of dough on a big butcher block table in the centre of the room.'

'Ornery old billy-goat,' Clay said. 'He can't wait to be the bearer of bad tidings. He knows how I feel about that by now.' He gave Jennifer a wry little smile.

'I hope I'm not the cause of some friction between you,' Jennifer said anxiously.

Clay shook his head. 'Not at all. Friction's the name of the game with Clarence. He's got his ways, and I have mine, but we usually meet somewhere in the middle.' He pushed the chair next to the one where he sat at the head of the table out with one foot, and then stretched his long legs out and put his stockinged feet up on the chair seat. 'That's better,' he said with a sigh and a satisfied smile. 'Walking a couple of miles through deep snow is awfully hard on the old legs.' He turned his head. 'Cookie,' he called back over his shoulder, 'how about another cup of coffee for me and one for Jenny?'

While the coffee was brought, Jennifer waited nervously, thinking that perhaps now she was going to be on the receiving end of instructions from Clayton Cooper about how she was to perform her new job. She doubted he would mince any words about exactly what he expected. Instead, Clay took a drink of his coffee and then gave her a smile that was so warm and intimate that she almost felt like blushing.

'Well, Jenny, my girl,' he said, 'how do you like life at the Bar-C so far? You've been called to do just about everything but what you came here for.'

'Th-that's certainly true,' she replied, and then she did blush in embarrassment at stammering like a silly schoolgirl. 'But I do like it,' she added, thinking as she did so that she sounded a great deal like someone who could neither add nor subtract.

'Even though it's not what you expected?' Clay asked, a twinkle joining the glowing warmth in his eyes.

'Yes, even though,' Jennifer agreed, wishing that her brain would start functioning with its normal precision instead of feeling as if it were suffering from some kind of short circuit in the wiring. 'But I'm really looking forward to getting to work on your books and records,' she added, then stared, wide-eyed, at Clay, who threw back his head and laughed. 'I don't understand what's so funny, Mr Cooper,' she said, frowning. 'I did come here to be your accountant.'

'Of course you did,' he replied with a grin. 'But my name's Clay, and no one in their right mind would really be looking forward to getting into that mess.'

'Then I guess maybe I am a little odd,' Jennifer said, smiling weakly. 'I do like to do accounting work. It's the only thing that I do really well.'

'I sincerely doubt that,' Clay replied, 'but I guess I can understand why someone might like it. Sort of like bringing order out of chaos. Gives you a feeling of accomplishment.'

'That's right,' Jennifer agreed. 'But I can't imagine that your books are in a state of chaos, as successful as you are.'

Clay shrugged. 'It looks like chaos to me, but maybe I just don't understand the system the last fellow used. I'm hoping that you can come up with something that makes more sense to me. I've had to keep my own separate system going in my head, just so I'd have some idea where I stood.'

'Oh, I'm sure I can do that,' Jennifer said quickly. 'With a computer and a printer I can have everything at your fingertips whenever you want to see it.'

'That's exactly what I want,' Clay said with a nod. 'I'll let you have a go at it in a day or two. First, though——'

'But, Mr Cooper——'

'Clay.'

'Clay. Tax time is almost here. I'd better get started right away,' Jennifer said frowning. Apparently, her new boss had little idea of the amount of time tax preparation could take.

'Now, don't get all wrought up over that,' Clay said, shaking his head. 'You're probably going to need an assistant, and I've got someone in mind, but I want you to understand the ranch first, or you won't have any idea what some of the items are all about. I know there's some way you can put those taxes off for a while. You'd better do that.'

'Well, I suppose I can file for an extension,' Jennifer said dubiously.

Clay smiled. 'That's the idea. Now, first thing in the morning we'll go for a ride——'

'Mr Cooper—Clay—I don't ride,' Jennifer interrupted, feeling very small as Clay frowned and looked amazed at the same time. 'I fell off a horse and broke my arm when I was little,' she explained, hoping for a more sympathetic response. She got nothing of the kind.

'It's past time you got back on a horse, then,' Clay said positively. 'Don't you worry, I'll give you a nice gentle one, and we'll only be walking them around the area here. That way, you'll be used to being on horseback again by the time the snow melts. There's a lot of pretty scenery I want to show you, and there's no other way to get there.'

Jennifer swallowed and said nothing. The idea of getting on a horse terrified her. Maybe she'd be lucky and fall down the stairs and break a leg in the morning. Then again, Clayton Cooper might put her on a horse, cast and all. She could tell by the way he was looking at her that he had decided that she was going to get on a horse if he had to put her there and tie her on to it. As if he could read her mind, he smiled at her suddenly.

'I know you're scared,' he said, 'but you'll be fine. I'll take good care of you.' He swung his feet to the floor and stood up. 'I think I'll turn in now. I've been up since four this morning. You're welcome to stay up and read or play the piano or anything you like. I want you to feel that this is your home.'

'Thank you,' Jennifer said, feeling awkward under Clay's intense gaze as she also stood up. 'I think I may as well go to my room now, too. I've got some more unpacking to do.'

She immediately regretted her decision, for it meant that she and Clay climbed the stairs together, and then walked down the hall side by side until they came to their doors on the opposite sides of the hall.

'Well—uh—goodnight,' she said, giving him a tentative little smile as they both paused in the hallway.

'Goodnight, Jenny,' Clay said, his deep voice soft and

warm. He cocked his head and looked at her thoughtfully. 'Do I make you nervous?' he asked.

'Oh, no,' she said quickly, although she felt so tense that her upper lip was perspiring. 'I think I'm just a little slow at . . . at adjusting to so many new things all at once. I'm used to a very ordinary life in a little apartment in Chicago.'

'All alone?' Clay asked, still studying her intently. 'No boyfriends?'

'Well, one very persistent one that I'm . . . glad to get away from,' Jennifer answered, licking her lips nervously. Having Clay ask about her love-life was not making her feel any more relaxed. It really was none of his business.

'He wasn't mean to you, was he?'

Jennifer stared at him, startled by the question. Did she look that frightened? 'No, of course not,' she denied quickly. 'He was just . . . dull.' She was surprised by the look of relief on Clay's face.

'That's good,' he said. 'If there was one thing I wouldn't put up with, it'd be some bully mistreating my pretty little Jenny. I'd have hopped on the first plane for Chicago and given him a dose of his own medicine.' With a sudden impulsive move, Clay put his arms around Jennifer and pulled her close to him. 'Don't you worry about a thing. You're going to have a good time here, get lots of work done, and I promise it won't be dull.' He flashed a brilliant smile, gave Jennifer a quick kiss on the cheek, then released her. 'Goodnight, Jenny,' he said again. 'Set your alarm for six o'clock.' Then he turned and went quickly into his room.

CHAPTER TWO

JENNIFER went dazedly into her room, a vision of bright blue eyes and a wide smile in a tanned face framed by gold-streaked hair so vivid in her mind's eye that she scarcely saw her own room before her. Not until she stumbled over the suitcase she had left on the floor by her bed did she suddenly come out of her trance.

'Oh, my,' she murmured. She sat down on the edge of her bed and tried to analyse what had happened. Somewhere during the day, she decided, her expectations of what a wealthy rancher would be like had run smack into a very different reality. Clayton Cooper wasn't at all like she had imagined he would be, although he was definitely handsome. There was none of the stiff formality she had always found in the wealthy clients of Bailey and Scruggs. Of course, ranching was different from running a big corporation, a lot more down to earth. Perhaps it was the frequent contact with life and death that made Clay so open and lacking in ceremony. He hadn't really come at her like some prowling hunter in a singles bar, but wasn't it a little too informal for him to hug and kiss her and call her *his* Jenny?

Jennifer shook her head and stood up, still feeling wobbly. She had the strange impression that Clay's arms were still around her, strong and warm. There was a tingling sensation where his lips had touched her cheek. 'I'm going crazy,' she muttered to herself. Things like that only happened in storybooks. Real women didn't react to men that way. Which, Jennifer thought bemusedly, perhaps meant that she wasn't real. She wandered into her bathroom and stared into the mirror. No, she was still there, but she looked different. Her cheeks were pink and her eyes abnormally bright. Maybe she was coming down with something. She stuck out her tongue. It looked normal.

'I'd better go to bed,' she muttered. This day had obviously been too much for her. Too sudden a change. She took down her hair, stripped and showered, and felt a little better. Tomorrow, she thought, as she slipped her long flannel nightgown over her head, she would have to set Clayton Cooper straight on a few things. She did not want to get on a horse. If he wanted her to see the ranch, he could drive her around. He could learn that she wanted to be called Jennifer, not Jenny, and not *his* Jennifer, either. And she definitely did not want him to hug and kiss her. That was not a proper relationship between employer and employee. After breakfast, she would simply tell him those things in plain and simple English. If he didn't like it, he could fire her, and she would look for employment elsewhere.

Establishing a hypothetical plan of action made Jennifer feel more relaxed and in control. She climbed into the big, comfortable bed. The pillows were soft. Real goose down, she decided, snuggling against one. Clay did like nice things. He might be overly friendly, but he did seem to be a genuinely kind person, strong and authoritative, but not in the least crude or unpleasant. If she told him about Alan Bailey, would he really fly to Chicago to avenge her? She smiled to herself. Now that would be something to see! Imagining that delightful scene, she drifted off to sleep.

Her alarm had not yet gone off when a scraping noise

on the balcony outside her bedroom awakened her. It took her a few moments to realise that the sound she heard was someone pushing the snow off the balcony with a shovel, and to open her eyes and discover that it was just getting light outside. She sat up and looked towards the windows, then jumped, startled, at the sight of a face appearing in one window. Clay's face. He pressed his nose to the window, saw Jennifer, then grinned and disappeared. A moment later he tapped on her door.

'Good lord,' Jennifer muttered. 'Does he think I'm going to invite him in?' He was definitely pushing this instant friendship too far. She pulled on her robe, thrust her feet into her slippers, and went to the door. 'What do you want?' she grumbled, frowning at him through a narrow crack. 'It's not time to get up yet.'

'Come out here for a minute,' he said. He pushed the door open and scooped her through it with one arm around her shoulders. 'Look.' He pointed towards the east.

Jennifer looked, then let out her breath in a long 'Ooooh.' The sun had not yet risen above the mountain peaks, but its light had ignited their snowy tops with a rosy glow that changed from moment to moment as the sun rose higher. 'I never saw anything so beautiful,' she whispered, entranced. She looked up at Clay and smiled. 'I'm sorry I was cross. It's magnificent.'

'That's better,' he said, treating her to another of those smiles that had dazzled her the night before. 'I thought for a minute there that you were going to bite me.'

'I'm not at my best when I first wake up,' Jennifer said, looking quickly back at the sky. The colours continued to change, slowly fading. Golden shafts shot upwards from the sun. Closer by, a cow mooed, a horse whickered, and a jay streaked by, squawking, towards the pines.

'The world is waking up,' Clay said softly. He gave Jennifer's shoulders a squeeze. 'You'd better get back inside before you get chilled. I wanted you to see that sunrise. I thought it might help you understand why I love the Bar-C so much. My mama used to say that the first time she saw a sunrise like that she thought she'd died and gone to heaven.'

Jennifer could feel the note of intense passion in Clay's voice and see it in his face as he gazed out across the valley. 'I can certainly understand why she did,' she said. She looked up at Clay again. 'I didn't think I'd ever thank anyone for waking me up, but I'm glad that you did. I think I'll set my alarm to see that every morning.'

'It's a good way to start the day,' Clay agreed. He smiled slowly, his eyes sleepily warm as they drifted to Jennifer's lips and then back to her eyes. 'I'll see you at breakfast,' he said. 'Dress warmly. You'd better put on some long johns.' He opened Jennifer's door for her and waited while she turned stiffly and went inside. She heard him whistling as he went back along the balcony to his own room.

For several minutes, Jennifer stood still in the middle of her room, her arms clasped tightly around her, waiting for her speeding pulse to slow down and her mind to regain control of her wayward emotions. Clayton Cooper had done it to her again, she thought grimly, and she did not like it. One minute he was a man of passion and warmth towards his land and his animals, and the next he was an outrageous flirt! He might not have time to chase women, but it looked as if he had hired her so that he could have his fun without leaving home. There was certainly every indication that he had more in mind for her than accounting. Well, he could just forget whatever it was! Jennifer Tarkinton had not come all the way to Montana to become his combination accountant and mistress, if that was what he was planning. He was wealthy and handsome enough to find himself plenty of female companions who would be happy to come and live in his beautiful house and be his playmate for a while.

'He's going to get an earful if he tries anything,' Jennifer vowed in a muttered soliloquy, as she rummaged for her aerobics tights, which would have to substitute for long johns. 'I didn't expect it to be so cold this time of year. I suppose if I stay I'll have to get some long underwear. But I'm not going to stay, if that man doesn't stop looking at me like that. It makes me too nervous. I feel like a mouse about to be pounced on by a great, smiling tiger.'

She got dressed, put her hair up in its usual topknot, then took her down-filled jacket and a stocking cap and scarf with her as she went downstairs to breakfast. She was trying for a resolutely stern expression which would brook no nonsense, but it failed completely in the face of Pam's enthusiastic, 'Hi, Jennifer!' and the friendly greetings from the cowboys, who were already at the breakfast table.

'This here's Barkley,' the man named Flint said, elbowing his neighbour and grinning at Jennifer. 'He don't usually come to breakfast, but he wanted to see the pretty new accountant.'

'Hello, Barkley. I'm glad to meet you,' Jennifer said, smiling at the thin, middle-aged man who looked embarrassed and only briefly glanced at her and muttered, 'How do?' Clarence was certainly right, she thought, at least as far as the Bar-C was concerned, that most of the working cowhands weren't young. All of them looked weatherbeaten and tough, something in their appearance reminding her of wild, free creatures who would rather die than be caged. Perhaps there was something to that song that warned against marrying a cowboy. Of course, Clarence and Nell seemed happy enough, by maybe they were exceptional.

Clay was not yet at the table. Jennifer helped carry in baskets of fresh scones and jars of honey, and then took her place. In the distance she could hear the sound of someone playing a Mozart piano sonata. Perhaps, she thought, Clay liked to listen to music and catch up on some of his reading before breakfast. She sometimes did that herself.

Pam finished her breakfast and jumped up from the table. 'Who's going to take me to the bus?' she asked.

'I'll do it,' answered one of the hands. 'I've got to go that way to pick up some feed, anyway.'

'OK. I'll get my stuff and say goodbye to Uncle Clay,' Pam replied, and scurried off

Jennifer could hear Pam's footsteps charging up the stairs, then back down a few moments later. Then the Mozart suddenly stopped, replaced by a loud fanfare, and then one finger picking out 'tum tum ta dum dum— tum tum'. Good heavens, that had been Clay playing, with those huge, strong hands that looked as if they had been bruised and broken in many a tangle with a wayward cow or horse. She wouldn't have believed it possible. She heard Pam, say, 'See you later,' and then giggle as if she were bring tickled. 'Uncle Clay said I killed his cadenza,' she said, still laughing, when she came back with her coat on and her book bag over her shoulder. She took the lunch box which Nell handed her as she hurried by, and then followed the cowhand through the back door, chattering happily about the day ahead.

'Kind of like watching a little whirlwind,' commented Clarence, with a smile. 'This place is sure a lot livelier with her around.' He lowered his voice. 'Used to be as quiet as a tomb after——' He stopped, his eyes focusing past Jennifer's shoulder on his boss's approaching form.

Jennifer stared at Clarence. 'After what?' she wanted to ask, but knew that whatever he had been about to say it was not something he would tell her in front of Clay.

Clay took his place at the head of the table and greeted everyone with a smile and a 'Good morning'. While he ate a hearty breakfast he discussed the day's agenda with Clarence, and Jennifer silently ate her two pieces of toast and wondered what it was that Clarence had been about to tell her. He had looked as if he was about to reveal some tragic secret. Was it something more to do with Clay's brother, or could Clay have once had a tragic love-affair, maybe even a wife who had met some terrible end? Clay didn't look like a man who had suffered such a loss, but you couldn't always tell. Having Pam to take care of might have helped erase any lingering sorrow. He seemed so devoted to the little girl.

At the sound of her name, Jennifer's attention returned to Clay's conversation, and she heard him enquiring after the calf they had revived the night before.

'Eating like a little pig,' Flint reported.

Clay grinned happily. 'We'll come and see him after a while,' he said. Then he looked at Jennifer and frowned. 'You'd better eat more than that,' he said, indicating her now empty plate. 'It's still pretty cold outside.'

Jennifer shook her head. 'That's the best I can do first thing in the morning, believe me. I'll survive.'

Clay looked unconvinced. 'Just barely,' he said drily. 'I'll have to get you out in the mountain air enough to improve your appetite and put some roses in your cheeks.'

'That sounds like a rerun of *Heidi*, with me as the pitiful Clara,' Jennifer replied coldly. Not only that, but it again sounded as if Clay was planning other activities than accounting for her, which reminded her of her resolution of the night before. She set her jaw and stared at Clay defiantly, trying to reprime herself for bringing up her complaints once Clarence and the other cowhands had left.

'It does, doesn't it?' Clay said, ignoring Jennifer's grouchiness and grinning at her. 'I read that to Pam once. She wanted me to buy her some goats right after that.' He turned back to Clarence and gave him a few last-minute instructions. Then Clarence and the remaining hands got up from the table, more or less in unison, and filed out through the kitchen. 'Come on, Jenny, let's get our things on and get moving, too,' Clay said, pushing his chair back from the table. 'Time's a-wasting.'

Jennifer nodded, but maintained a stolid silence. There was that 'Jenny' again. He was going to hear about that very shortly, but she was saving any further comments until they were outside, and she could make the points she had planned on out of earshot of anyone else. She zipped up her down jacket, pulled on her bright red stocking cap, and wound the matching scarf around her neck. A pair of fleece-lined leather gloves completed her outfit.

Clay looked her over and nodded approvingly. 'I like you in red,' he said. 'With your green eyes, you look like a Christmas present.' He held open the door, and then put his arm around Jennifer's shoulders as they went out on to the back porch.

'P-please don't do that,' Jennifer said, her voice not nearly as firm as she had planned it to be before Clay had told her she looked like a Christmas present.

'Do what?' Clay asked, keeping his arm around her as they went down the stairs and started walking along the drive which led past Clarence's house towards the horse barn in the distance.

He can't really not know what I mean, Jennifer thought, looking up at him and frowning. 'Don't put your arm around me,' she replied, this time sounding more cross than she'd intended. Clay jerked his arm away as if he had been burned.

'I didn't know you were a touch-me-not,' he said reprovingly. 'Or are you still afraid of me?'

'Certainly not,' Jennifer replied, although she found it impossible to maintain contact with his intensely blue eyes, and instead looked straight ahead as she added, 'It's just not proper. After all, I'm your employee, not your girlfriend. You certainly wouldn't do that with a male employee.'

Clay chuckled. 'No, I wouldn't. Are you accusing me of sexual harassment? That seems to be a popular phrase these days among the liberated ladies.'

'Well, I . . . I hadn't thought of it quite that way,' Jennifer replied, giving him a quick glance. 'I just felt that you were . . . overly friendly on such short acquaintance.'

At that, Clay roared with laughter. 'I'm sorry,' he said, grinning at Jennifer, who was staring at him, totally confused by his response. 'You're just such a cute little thing that I can't help wanting to hug you. I suppose where you come from if a man puts his arms around a woman the first time they meet it probably means he has only one thing in mind. With me, it just means that you make me feel warm and good inside, and I like to touch things that make me feel that way. In fact, every time I look at you I want to put both arms around you, and I'm afraid you're going to have to tie my hands behind my back to keep me from doing it for very long.' He grinned as Jennifer frowned at him. 'Maybe if you keep reminding me I'll get over it. Or maybe you'll figure out before then that I'm not going to assault you or try to seduce you. All right?'

'I—I guess so,' Jennifer replied, not at all sure how she felt about Clay's frank confession. She gave him a faint smile and then thrust her hands into her pockets and walked silently along beside him through the crunching snow. Knowing that Clay wanted to put his arms around her made her feel warm all over, in spite of the still wintery weather. No one had ever called her a cute little thing before. It made her feel breathless and giddy and sort of tingly all over. It was very disturbing, as if she had suddenly become someone entirely different from the rather proper and dignified Jennifer Tarkinton she was used to. She had known that Alan Bailey, and several men before him, had wanted to touch her, but she had never found that upsetting unless they had tried to carry out their desires against her wishes. It would be nice to think that what Clay had said and what she felt meant the beginning of something special, but it had happened so fast. How was she supposed to know what it meant?

'Jenny?' Clay said softly. When she looked up at him he smiled. 'You're awfully quiet. Did I say something wrong?'

'Not exactly,' she replied. 'I'm just not used to a man coming right out and saying what he feels like that.'

Clay shrugged. 'I figure life's too short to play games, Jenny,' he said. 'I guess I wouldn't fit very well into polite society. At least, that's what my brother tells me.'

Jennifer could see the distaste on Clay's face at this first mention he had made of his brother. For some reason, she felt personally offended that his brother would criticise him. 'Polite society isn't always so polite,' she said, the memory of the always mannerly Alan Bailey's *alter ego* still rankling. 'It can hide all kinds of nastiness.'

'Exactly what I meant, Jenny, my girl,' Clay said. His arm started towards her, but he quickly pulled it back, frowning at it as he did so.

Jennifer lowered her head to hide a smile. She knew that he was deliberately teasing her, but he did it so good-naturedly that it was impossible to be angry with him. The fact that he had called her Jenny once again reminded her that she had vowed to complain about that, too. She bit her lip. Should she? She might as well, as long as they were being honest with each other, although she was not sure how much good that would do either.

'There was one other thing I wanted to tell you,' she said, giving Clay a sideways look from beneath her lashes.

'Go ahead, shoot,' he said, his eyes crinkling into a warm smile. 'I can take it.'

'I'd prefer to be called Jennifer,' she said. 'A jenny's a female mule. And don't tell me that it fits,' she added, seeing Clay's smile broaden into a grin.

Clay laughed. 'But a jenny wren is also an adorable little bird with a lovely voice,' he said. 'Couldn't you think of yourself as that kind of a jenny? Somehow,

Jenny seems to me to fit you better than Jennifer. It's more dainty and feminine.'

Jennifer felt her cheeks grow warm again. Clay was so very good at turning a graceful compliment and undoing all of her resolutions. 'I suppose I could try,' she murmured. 'It's not worth arguing over.'

'There, you see?' Clay said. 'You just proved you're not a jenny mule.' He gave Jennifer's shoulders a quick squeeze, and then pretended to grasp his own arm and hold it against his side. 'Darn thing,' he said, frowning. 'It's making me feel like Dr Strangelove.'

The twinkle in Clay's eyes was irresistible. Jennifer laughed and shook her head at the same time. 'Are you sure you're really Clayton Cooper, owner of the Bar-C Ranch?' she asked. 'You don't act at all like I thought a cattle baron would.'

'Nell tells me I'm thirty-five, going on seventeen,' Clay replied, grinning. 'Yes, ma'm, I am a gen-u-ine cattle baron. I hope you didn't think I'd be as dull as that fellow you left behind. Or are you trying to tell me that I'm not dignified enough?' He straightened his shoulders and looked down at her from beneath his thick, sandy-coloured lashes. 'There are some people in that so-called polite society who think I am an absolute paragon of dignity. Of course, I'm as dull as dirt then, too, because I'm bored to tears. Take your pick.'

Jennifer shook her head again. 'I think I'd rather get used to thirty-five, going on seventeen. But it might take me a while.'

'I understand,' Clay said, his face suddenly sympathetic. 'You're getting a whole lot of new things thrown at you all at once. Just take one day at a time and you'll have it all assimilated before you know it.'

They had reached the paddocks adjoining the horse

barn. Clay stopped, and made an encompassing gesture towards the barn and paddocks.

'The horses we keep here,' he said, 'are special. It's a separate enterprise from the cattle company. We raise and train fine cutting horses, and sell them to ranches all over the west. We've even sold some to foreign ranchers. It's kept separate for accounting and tax purposes. It gets complicated because some of the men work part time for both outfits, and some of the upkeep expenses have to be portioned out of the supplies we buy for the ranch in general. Think you can handle something like that all right?'

'Of course,' Jennifer replied. 'I worked with a farmer who invented a new piece of forage harvesting equipment, and then incorporated a separate company to produce it right on his farm.'

'Did you, now?' Clay said, looking impressed, which made Jennifer wonder if he had actually thought that, in spite of her experience, she really couldn't add or subtract. He turned at the sound of a heavy gate being raised, as a beautiful black horse was let out into the high, sturdily fenced paddock next to them. 'Say hello to Coal King,' he said, whistling softly to the horse, who kicked up his heels and then came prancing through the snow to the fence. 'He's our present stallion. First one we've had that was born here at the Bar-C, and the best.'

Clay's pride was obvious, and the horse was beautiful to look at, but Jennifer felt her anxiety over riding return at the sight of the huge, spirited animal.

'He's certainly . . . beautiful,' she said. 'Do you ride him?'

'Once in a while,' Clay replied. 'He can be pretty cantankerous, though. He's not a horse for an inexperienced rider. And stallions can be very unpredictable. Don't ever climb into the pen with him just because he's pretty and looks friendly.'

'I wouldn't think of it,' Jennifer said weakly.

Clay gave her a knowing look. 'Now,' he said, taking her arm and starting towards the barn, 'as to what you're going to ride today——'

'Oh, please, Clay,' Jennifer said, 'couldn't we just drive around and see things? I'm not ready to get on a horse.'

'You'll never be any readier than you are now,' Clay said firmly, 'and putting it off will only make it harder. Just relax. The horse I'm going to put you on is about as spirited as a rocking-chair. She's eighteen years old, and her name is Midnight. She's the mother of Coal King. She was given to me on my seventeenth birthday, and I brought her up right. She knows everything there is to know about how to behave like a lady. She'll understand almost everything you say to her.'

'What if I tell her that I'm terrified of her?' Jennifer asked, blinking and trying to adjust her eyes to the darkness of the horse barn after the brilliance of the sun on the snow.

'Then she'll be extra careful,' Clay replied. 'There she is now. She heard my voice,' he said, pointing to a black head, peering out of a stall towards them, ears pricked forward. He stopped in front of her and smiled. 'Hello, love,' he said, and the horse rubbed her soft, somewhat greyed muzzle against his neck, seeming to kiss him with her lips. 'That's my good old gal,' he said, caressing her fondly. 'Would you like to take this pretty little lady for a ride, Midnight?' The horse nodded her head up and down. 'See,' Clay said, grinning at Jennifer. 'She's looking forward to it.'

Jennifer stared at the horse and then back at Clay,

amazed. 'How did she know what you said?'

'Didn't I tell you that Midnight understands what you say? She's the smartest horse in the world. She knows everything there is to know about me, so if some time you want to find out my darkest secrets, just ask Middie. The only rule is to ask her yes-no questions and end with her name. Just try it. Stand close, so she can hear you.'

'All right,' Jennifer said sceptically, moving in front of Midnight. 'Do you know that I'm terrified of riding, Midnight?' she asked. 'Good heavens, she does understand!' she exclaimed when the horse again nodded.

'Told you so,' Clay said smugly. He reached for the bridle, which was hanging by the stall, slid the bit into Midnight's mouth, and tucked the headpiece behind her ears. 'Open the gate,' he instructed Jennifer. When she had done so, he handed her the reins. 'Lead her on out,' he said, 'then just wait here while I get my horse. I'll show you how to put a saddle on.'

Faced with the prospect of either doing as she was told or looking like a completely cowardly fool, Jennifer led the old horse into the centre of the barn and stopped. 'You are a sweet old lady, aren't you, Midnight?' she said, patting the horse's neck with a trembling hand. Midnight nodded again and then nuzzled Jennifer's neck. Jennifer sighed. 'I guess if I've got to ride a horse, I'm glad it's you,' she said resignedly. So far her score at getting Clay to do what she wanted instead of what he wanted was exactly zero. He wasn't unpleasant about it. He simply dodged and wove around anything that wasn't on his agenda, and ended up exactly where he had planned to be. Perhaps, Jennifer thought, that was what Clarence had meant when he'd said that Clay was 'particular'. He wanted things done his way, full stop.

She hoped fervently that when it came to accounting Clay didn't have too many ideas of his own about how he wanted her to do her job. She had her own way of doing things, and would get things organised so he could understand them perfectly. But, if he interfered——

Jennifer's musings were interrupted by Clay leading a big bay gelding down the centre of the barn. 'We'll tie them at the end, and then I'll show you the tack-room,' he said. In a short time, he had shown Jennifer the saddles and other supplies that were part of the depreciable inventory of the horse operation.

'There's a lot to keep track of on this ranch,' Clay commented. 'I never was sure old McDonald was doing it right.'

'I hope he was,' Jennifer said, thinking of the thousands of depreciable items that must be involved. 'Did he do an annual inventory?'

Clay pushed back his hat and scratched his head. 'I'm not sure. He got all of the bills, so he must have had a pretty good idea about it.'

'Oh, great,' Jennifer said, with a wry twist of her mouth. 'That sounds like something I'll have to check out right away.'

'Don't be afraid to ask for help on that,' Clay said. 'Now let's get you trained-up on saddling a horse.'

He brought out their saddles, and instructed Jennifer on how to put one on Midnight, insisting that she do most of it herself. After he had put the saddle on his horse, whose name was Ace, they led the horses outside.

'All right, up you go,' he said, coming to give Jennifer a helping hand. 'Just put your foot in the stirrup and I'll give you a boost this first time.'

Midnight suddenly looked twice as big as she had

moments before to Jennifer. She eyed the stirrup and licked her lips nervously, terror seizing her anew. 'Do I have to?' she asked, looking pleadingly at Clay.

'Well, let's see,' Clay said, pulling thoughtfully on his chin. A spark of sheer devilment suddenly lit his eyes. 'Tell you what, Jenny, my girl, I'll drive you around in the pick-up *if* you'll let me put my arms around you . . . and kiss you.'

'I—I'll ride,' she said hoarsely, blushing as Clay roared with laughter.

'I thought that might do the trick,' he said. He boosted Jennifer into the saddle, adjusted her stirrups, showed her how to hold the reins, and then swung easily on to his horse. He made a little clucking sound. Both horses moved off together.

At first, Jennifer was too tense to do anything but cling to the pommel and reins at the same time, expecting any moment that she would either faint and fall under the horse's hoofs or make some move that would convince old Midnight that she should throw this miserable, shaking person from her back. She was afraid to turn her head when Clay called her attention to something, only nodding dumbly at his comments. When they had passed the last of the buildings and were on the road which led to the ranch gate, Jennifer at last spoke.

'I thought we were just going to ride around where the buildings are,' she said plaintively.

'We were,' Clay replied, 'but I think we'd better just keep on going until you relax, even if it means we ride all of the way into Bozeman. Of course, at this rate that might take until tomorrow, but we'll get there. Now, take a deep breath, close your eyes, and just feel the horse underneath you. Let your body go limp and rock along with the motion instead of fighting it.'

Jennifer shot Clay a desperate look, but he only smiled encouragingly, like a patient parent dealing with a backward child. One who was quite capable of taking her all of the way to Bozeman if necessary. She took a deep breath and did as he had told her. Midnight walked daintily along, picking her way carefully down the still snowy road. Gradually, Jennifer relaxed and felt the gentle rocking motion. It was almost hypnotising. She let her head fall forwards.

'Hey, don't go to sleep. Open your eyes now,' Clay said, laughing. 'That's much better. Keep that up and we'll turn around at the gate.'

'It's not so bad now,' Jennifer said, taking another deep breath. She looked around. Something seemed different. 'What's that I smell?' she asked. 'It's like . . . I don't know. Can something smell soft?'

'It's nice to know that you're breathing again,' Clay teased. 'I think what you smell is the change in the air. I noticed it when we started out. I think spring's decided to come our way. I doubt the snow will last more than another day or two down here.'

'Spring,' Jennifer said thoughtfully. 'That's what it is. Will it get really warm here soon?'

'Not for quite a while,' Clay replied, 'but with any luck we won't have any more snow at this altitude. And in a few weeks I'll be able to show you mountain valleys full of wild flowers. That's a sight you'll never forget.'

'It sounds lovely,' Jennifer said, although her enthusiasm was tempered by the realisation that getting to those valleys probably implied more horseback riding. She was beginning to feel more comfortable, but still a long way from being confident.

'Let's turn back,' Clay said, when they reached the

ranch gate. 'I think you've saved us that trip to
Bozeman. As soon as the snow's gone, we'll start some
serious riding instruction. Before long, you'll be finding
old Midnight too tame for your taste.'

'I seriously doubt that,' Jennifer said, as they turned
and started back. 'Besides, I wouldn't want to abandon
her. It might hurt her feelings.'

When they reached the long, low building where the
unmarried cowhands lived, Clay brought Ace to a halt
and dismounted. 'Let's visit our orphaned calf,' he said.

'My goodness, did Ken and Flint have to take him
right into their apartment?' Jennifer asked, waiting for
Clay to help her down from Midnight.

Clay laughed. 'No, but they would have if necessary.
That's happened before. But a couple of years ago I built
on a nursery-room, just for such emergencies. Come on,
put your weight on your left stirrup, swing your right
leg over and get down. Unless you're that anxious for
me to put my arms around you again.'

'Oh, all right,' Jennifer grumbled, glaring as he
grinned at her. Clay was certainly using that threat
overtime. She was beginning to wish she hadn't
mentioned anything about it. She got down rather
awkwardly, and then received instructions on looping
the reins over a fence rail. 'It's beginning to seem as if
I came here to attend a riding school instead of taking a
job,' she commented crossly. She felt bow-legged from
sitting on Midnight's plump back, and her empty
stomach was beginning to growl in protest.

'I told you you should have eaten more breakfast,'
Clay said when he heard it. 'Ruins a person's
disposition, going around hungry half of the time.'

Jennifer said nothing as she followed Clay towards
the back of the building, but she was having plenty of

dire thoughts about one Clayton Cooper, who obviously thought he knew everything there was to know about everything. Maybe she should just tell him she'd decided she'd made a mistake and quit before they really tangled.

There was a small shed attached to the back of the building, with a pen along one side of it. Clay went through the pen and opened the door of the shed, letting Jennifer go ahead of him. Ken was already there, holding a bottle for the calf, who was standing and drinking eagerly, his little tail flicking happily back and forth.

'Oh, bless his heart, he looks so healthy and strong!' Jennifer exclaimed. 'It's already hard to believe he's the same calf.' She looked up at Clay, and caught on his face a look of such intense happiness that she could not tear her eyes away. He looked, she thought, as happy as a proud father at the hospital nursery window. He caught her watching him and smiled.

'This is what makes it all worth while,' he said, his voice husky with emotion. 'Sometimes you stay up all night and try everything you can think of, and they don't respond, but when they do . . . it's something special. Isn't it, Ken?'

The cowhand nodded, caressing the calf's soft little head with a leathery hand, a gentle smile on his face. 'Ain't nothin' like it,' he said.

The calf noisily finished his bottle and then wobbled towards Jennifer on his still uncertain legs. She squatted and petted him, laughing when he leaned against her and she lost her balance and sat down in the straw. 'You're a pretty husky guy already,' she said, getting to her knees and hugging him around the neck. 'Keep eating like that and you'll be chasing the lady cows around the pasture in no time.'

'Not for very long, he won't,' Ken said drily. 'He'll become a steer in a couple of months.'

'Poor baby,' Jennifer said, frowning. 'It's a good thing he can't understand such things. Does that hurt them a lot?'

'Not as much as you might think,' Clay said, dropping to one knee beside her and rubbing the calf's ears. 'Cattle have a very good supply of endorphins, which is the name for the natural analogue of morphine that most animals, including humans, have in their system. When they first feel pain, the endorphins are released. That keeps them from suffering too much.'

'Nature provides,' Ken said, nodding.

'That's good to know,' Jennifer said, feeling a little twinge of guilt for having thought Clay was a know-it-all. He really did know so many things that were entirely new to her.

She watched Clay as he stroked the calf and felt it all over, like a doctor examining a patient. His face was serious now, totally absorbed in what his gentle hands were telling him about the calf's condition. When he had finished, and all was apparently well, he laid his cheek against the calf's soft neck and closed his eyes for a moment. Quite suddenly, it was all that Jennifer could do to keep from reaching out and caressing his golden hair. He looked so young and vulnerable, and at the same time so strong, as if he held some ancient wisdom that made him one with the world around him. How could that be? What a complex and confusing man he was. Then he opened his eyes and smiled at her, and she knew in that instant that she was not going to leave the Bar-C.

CHAPTER THREE

THE regular cowhands had already finished lunch and departed when Clay and Jennifer arrived back at the ranch house.

'Sorry we're late. Got anything left for us?' Clay asked Nell, who shook her head and smiled wryly at Jennifer.

'As if I expected him to be on time,' she said. 'He knows perfectly well your lunch is waiting.'

Clay looked hurt. 'Now, Nell, I'm on time every now and then,' he said. 'Besides, Jenny's so hungry that I'm not sure there'll be enough for two of us. We've got to get her trained to eat breakfast.'

Jennifer frowned. 'Will you please stop harping on my eating habits? If I'd known we were going to be gone so long, I'd have taken along a sandwich.'

'Tch, tch,' Clay clucked. 'Still cross as a bear. Sure hope food improves your disposition.'

'I am not——' Jennifer began, and then stopped before she could prove Clay right. Something was making her more edgy than usual, but she wasn't sure whether it was hunger for food or that nameless longing that had invaded her while she'd watched Clay with the orphaned calf. It made her feel vaguely uneasy, as if she had come home to discover her apartment had been ransacked, but could find nothing missing. 'I'm starved,' she said instead, the sight of a huge bowl of homemade beef and vegetable soup making her mouth water. Maybe she was just extra hungry, after all. She

61

devoured two bowls of soup and several hot scones with butter and honey, avoiding looking at Clay, who was wearing an I-told-you-so expression.

'Are you finally going to show me the office this afternoon?' she asked, to forestall any comments on the large piece of cherry pie with which she was finishing off her lunch.

Clay shook his head. 'You'll be too sleepy after being out in the cold and then eating all that lunch to do any brain work. We'll just take a little siesta for about half an hour and then I'm going to drive you to the cow camp where I was yesterday. There are a few things I still want you to know about before you start in.' He grinned as Jennifer frowned at him. 'Don't you worry, I'll let you at those books tomorrow. Now let's take that siesta, so you'll be rarin' to go again.'

'If I go to sleep now, I'll be groggy all afternoon,' Jennifer said, still frowning. 'You go ahead. I'll read or something.'

'You've got to learn some better habits,' Clay replied, a teasing twinkle in his eyes. 'Come on. There are two sofas in the living-room. You take one and I'll take the other. I guarantee you'll feel like a million if you take a little nap.'

Jennifer opened her mouth to protest and then closed it again. She might as well pretend to go along with Clay. She could lie on the sofa and read a magazine while he dozed.

'That's better,' Clay said, grinning as Jennifer stood up and gave him a defiant look. He put an arm around her shoulders and started towards the living-room. 'Oops, darn, I forgot,' he said, removing his arm in response to her glare.

'You're not the only one who needs to learn better

habits,' she said tightly. She might as well have said nothing at all about his putting his arm around her, for all the good it had done. She sat down on the first sofa and picked up a magazine from the coffee-table in front of it. 'I doubt I'll be able to sleep,' she said, in response to Clay's reproving look.

'You sure won't if you're reading that,' he said, taking hold of the magazine and trying to pull it from her hands. 'Come on. Just lie down and shut your eyes.'

'No!' Jennifer said stubbornly. She was not going to knuckle under to every weird idea Clay had. She held on to the magazine so tightly that she was pulled to her feet. 'I'll read a magazine if I want to! ' she snapped. 'Let go.' She tried futilely to jerk the magazine from Clay's hands. Instead, he easily wrenched it from her grasp and tossed it over his shoulder. Jennifer's usually even temper boiled over. 'You are the most obnoxious, stubborn, unreasonable man I've ever met!' she cried, pummelling his chest with her fists. 'Either you stop trying to push me around or I'm not going to stay and work for you!'

'Jenny,' Clay said softly, ignoring her fists and putting his arms around her loosely, 'I'm not trying to push you around. I'm just trying to help you get used to living a different kind of life from what you're used to. Now, we got up very early and were out in that cold air for a long time before we had that big lunch. You're going to feel a lot better if you take a little nap and digest your food before we go out in the cold again.'

Jennifer stood perfectly still in the circle of Clay's arms. While he'd spoken her fists had come to rest quietly against his broad chest. She'd listened to his deep voice, hypnotised by the changeable currents that made his blue eyes, locked intently on to hers, seem first dark and then bright with an inner light. As he bent his head towards her, the deep lines that years of life in the outdoors had etched around his eyes crinkled along with the slow smile that came to his soft, generous mouth.

'You still mad at me?' he asked, a lock of golden hair falling across his forehead as he spoke.

Without thinking, Jennifer reached up and pushed the lock of hair back, and then let her hand follow on to rest behind Clay's neck. For the life of her, she could not remember why she had been so angry with him. His smile faded and he studied Jennifer's face carefully for a few moments. She could feel her pulse racing, but the rest of her being was suspended in time, waiting, waiting. Very slowly, he touched his parted lips to hers, and then hungrily moved his mouth across hers, kissing her repeatedly. The waiting ended, Jennifer's body trembled at the rush of excitement that streamed through her. She returned Clay's kisses eagerly, joining her hands behind his neck and holding him to her. If only he would hold her closer, so that she could feel him against her, feel him wanting this as much as she did. As if in answer to her thoughts, his arms tightened around her and a deep sound of pleasure came from his throat at her response.

'No, I guess you aren't,' he answered his own question as he raised his head again and smiled at Jennifer's dazed expression. 'Hold on tight, now.' He very gently picked her up and laid her on the sofa, then covered her with an afghan and tucked it around her. 'Have a good nap, beautiful green eyes,' he said, bending to kiss her lips again. He smiled, and then walked away.

Jennifer lay very still, staring at the criss-crosses of the beamed ceiling high above her. I can't believe what just happened, she thought. I must be dreaming. She had probably lain down, closed her eyes, and dozed off, imagining the whole thing. The Jennifer Tarkinton she knew would never let Clay kiss her like that, without a word of protest, in fact encouraging him every step of the way. She would not be lying here, still feeling as if she had drunk some kind of wonderful, magical potion that left her reeling, floating on a cloud that only looked like a sofa. She heard Clay give a luxurious sigh as he stretched out on the other sofa, which faced hers on the far side of the fireplace, the big, square coffee-table between them. She turned her head and looked towards him.

'Close those green eyes and go to sleep,' he said.

No, she hadn't been dreaming. Clay was still there, still ordering her around as if he owned her. 'Go to sleep yourself!' she snapped, and then returned her attention to the ceiling, ignoring his deep, throaty chuckle. What an impossibly egotistical man! He thought that the fact that she had kissed him meant that she didn't mean anything she'd said about him behaving himself in a more appropriate manner. Well, it didn't! He did seem to have some unexplainable power over her, but she could learn to overcome that. She had better. For all she knew, he was planing to go just as far as she would let him. Maybe further. How could she tell whether behind his apparently warm, open friendliness there lurked another Alan Bailey? He was planning to take her for a long drive this afternoon . . .

At that thought, Jennifer turned to face the back of the sofa and shut her eyes, suddenly so tense that it hurt. I am not going to think about that, she vowed. I am not going to let Alan Bailey ruin the rest of my life. Clayton Cooper was nothing like him. Alan would never have cared for an orphaned calf as Clay did. She could still picture his face that morning, his beautiful smile. It made her feel warm, dreamy . . .

Clay's arm was around her. They were standing beside Coal King, who wore a gorgeous silver-trimmed saddle. Clay helped her up with him. They rode like the wind across endless fields of snow. Suddenly, she looked back at him and he had changed. His hair was dark, and he was wearing a business suit. It was Alan! His eyes were cold and cruel. He reined in the horse and pressed his lifeless lips to hers while his hands tore at her clothes . . .

'No! Don't!' Jennifer cried. She sat bolt upright, her heart racing, at the sensation of someone shaking her shoulders. 'Oh, thank goodness, it's you,' she said, fighting down the chill panic of her nightmare. Clay was sitting beside her, peering anxiously into her face. She stared at him, trying to erase the image of Alan leering at her, the sensation of his clammy hands on her skin. 'I was having a bad dream,' she said shakily, rubbing her hand across her eyes. 'I'm all right now.'

Clay's eyes searched Jennifer's intently. 'You were saying "No, don't!" and waving your arms as if you were trying to push someone away. What happened, Jenny? Was it something real that comes back in your dreams?'

'Yes,' Jennifer said tightly, 'but it's nothing important. I don't want to talk about it.' She had told no one else what Alan had done, passing off her blackened eye as an accidental bump.

Clay took Jennifer's chin between his fingers. When she jerked it away he put his arms around her and forced her head down against his shoulder. 'Take it easy,' he said, his hand massaging across her tight shoulders.

'Don't be afraid. Some man did attack you, didn't he? Don't be afraid to tell me. I won't think any less of you, and it might help to talk about it.'

The warm, sympathetic sound of Clay's voice was too much for Jennifer. She began to sob.

'Poor little love,' he said, patting her back. 'Poor little darling.'

Jennifer gulped back her sobs and shook her head. 'It's just stupid of me,' she said, raising her head to look at Clay. 'I wasn't really attacked, Clay, not like you're thinking. I got a little shaking and a slap, that's all. I don't know why it bothers me at all any more. Maybe because it was such a shock. I thought I knew the man. I never suspected he'd do anything like that when I told him not to . . . to paw me. But he'd had a few drinks too many. It changed him.'

Clay nodded soberly. 'I understand. It can be a terrible shock when you find out a person isn't what you thought they were. Believe me, I know. But after a while it fades away. Good things come and push it to the back of your mind.' He traced Jennifer's cheek with his fingertip. 'I'd never hurt you, Jenny,' he said. 'I hope my kissing you like that isn't what triggered your dream. Do I remind you of——?'

'Good heavens, no!' Jennifer interrupted. 'You don't look like him, you don't act like him, you don't——' She stopped just in time to prevent herself from saying 'kiss like him'. 'Never mind,' she said, as Clay cocked his head and looked at her curiously.

'Jenny,' Clay said, a teasing gleam coming into his eyes, 'tell me what else it is that I "don't" do like him. Come on, now. I'll spend the rest of the day trying to guess if you don't.'

'I said never mind,' she repeated, her cheeks growing

warm under Clay's amused scrutiny.

'Don't smell like him?' he guessed. When Jenny only pursed her mouth tightly he laughed. 'Don't feel like him?' he persisted. 'Don't sound like him, don't eat like him? Jenny, don't be so cruel,' he said, his forehead puckered in exaggerated anguish. 'Tell me before I go crazy.'

'You *are* crazy,' Jennifer said, starting to giggle at Clay's ridiculous face. 'I haven't . . . had a fit like this . . . in years,' she choked out, trying desperately to stop, and each time failing. Finally she succeeded, heaving a sigh of relief, but feeling wonderfully light-hearted, none the less. In all the time she had known Alan Bailey, she could never recall having laughed uncontrollably at anything he had said or done. He would certainly never have stooped to making ridiculous faces in order to make her laugh. 'You're absolutely nothing like him,' she said. 'In any way.'

Clay grinned. 'I think that's probably good,' he said. 'Now will you tell me?'

Jennifer made a face. 'You don't kiss like him.'

'And is *that* good?'

You know it is, Jennifer thought. Why bother to ask? She studied Clay's face thoughtfully. He looked carefree and confident enough on the surface, still smiling, but deep in his eyes she thought she saw something else, a fear that came from whoever it was who had disappointed him so badly. Perhaps the person of the time when this house of laughter had been as silent as a tomb still cast a shadow over this man who loved his home, his animals and little Pam with such deep, unashamed warmth. Maybe he, too, needed reassuring that Jennifer Tarkinton was really the person she seemed, and had felt what he thought she'd felt from his kiss. But should she tell him, and risk him concluding more from her confession than she'd like right now? Wavering, she bit her lip.

'That's all right,' Clay said gruffly. 'You don't have to answer that one.'

The disappointment in his face hit Jennifer like a physical blow and made her decision for her. 'I was wondering,' she said in gently scolding tones, 'why you had to ask. Of course that's good. Now could we please get on to some other subject? This one's making me nervous. Didn't you say we were going to one of the cow camps?'

'I did,' Clay said, glancing at his watch. 'And we'd better get moving.'

They put on their outdoor clothing again, and Clay led the way to a large metal shed near the horse barn, which sheltered stacks of square-baled hay and four pick-up trucks of assorted ages. 'We've got thirty pick-ups at the Bar-C,' he told Jennifer. 'We used to replace half of them every year, but with profits down the past year we're keeping them going as long as possible. I'd planned to replace one of our big cattle trucks this year, but that's going to have to wait, too, I'm afraid.'

'Thirty pick-up trucks,' Jennifer murmured, as she got into the cab of a fairly new one. It was mind-boggling. She was definitely going to need help to keep track of everything.

It's a sort of roundabout way by road to the cow camp,' Clay said, as they turned on to the valley road. 'We have to go back to the highway and then go north. It's about thirty miles by road, but only a little over ten on horseback.'

'Does anyone live there?' Jennifer asked.

Clay chuckled. 'I forget I'm talking Greek to you half of the time. Yes, there's a family there full time, and a couple of extra hands there now. Jacob and Carrie Johnson and their five kids live there. Jacob's a veterinarian as well as a cowhand. He's in charge of the first-calf heifers that we herd into his area in the fall, so when they calve about this time of year they can be helped if necessary. You'll like the Johnsons. They're fine people.' He gestured towards the gate to the old Cooper ranch house which they were just passing. 'My brother, Forrest, lives there with my father. He was supposed to become the ranch vet, but he didn't take to vet school. Too much work. Now he's supposed to be our sales and marketing manager. Gives him a chance to put on his fancy clothes and look important.'

Jennifer looked over at Clay. It had been clear that Clarence disliked Forrest Cooper. Apparently Clay didn't think much of his brother, either, although his remarks had been made so matter-of-factly that his voice conveyed no rancour. 'I should think that would be a very important part of your operation,' she said. 'Is he good at that?'

'Good enough, I guess. We could use some more commercial contracts, though, instead of having so many go to auction.' He glanced over at Jennifer and grinned. 'More Greek. We don't feed calves out, we sell feeder calves. If we can sell large lots to commercial feedlots, the price is usually better. If you've got consistently good, healthy calves that are good gainers, which we have, the feedlots want them.'

'You sound as if you'd be a good salesman,' Jennifer commented.

Clay shook his head. 'Don't have the time, and I don't like it. Besides, I'm not half as good as Forrest when he turns on the charm.'

Jennifer frowned. 'He doesn't sound particularly charming to me. Clarence told me a little about him, including the fact that his wife left him because he chased other women.'

'Yeah, but wait until you see him,' Clay said drily. 'You'll probably change your tune. He looks like just what you think a cattle baron should look like. Wears custom suits, drives a fancy car. Knows which wine to serve with what.'

'Another Alan Bailey,' Jennifer said in disgusted tones. 'I hate him already.'

'So that's the guy's name,' Clay said. He reached over and gave Jennifer's hand a squeeze. 'Don't worry, Forrey won't bother you. I'll see to that. And, as far as I know, he's not a woman beater. I'm sure Tanya would have told me if he did anything like that. Tanya's his wife. She's not a bad sort. In fact, she's the person I was thinking of as your assistant. She's a good book-keeper, but not a real accountant. She used to assist our ex-accountant, so she probably has some idea how he had things organised. That might make it a little easier for you at first.'

'That would be a help,' Jennifer agreed. 'The more I learn about this place, the more I think I'm going to need at least one assistant, maybe more. It depends on how well organised your record-keeping is.'

Clay chuckled. 'It's not the greatest. I'm counting on you to track down all of our shortcomings and correct them.'

'That's exactly what I plan to do,' Jennifer said, 'but it might take a while.'

'As long as it's going to take for you to get used to me?' Clay asked, with a teasing twinkle in his eyes.

'Good heavens, I hope not!' Jennifer teased back, and Clay laughed delightedly.

'You're getting used to me already, Jenny, my girl. The way you pitched right in with that calf last night, I knew you were a fast learner.' He turned the truck on to a road which led along the north end of the valley. 'Now, before we get to the cow camp, let me tell you a little more about how they fit into the operation.'

For the rest of the drive, Clay described the work Jacob Johnson and the other hands who lived in cow camps did, keeping track of thousands of cattle, miles of fence, dozens of gates. At the Johnsons' warm little home Jennifer got a first-hand look at the lives of those hard-working people, whose devotion to the cattle and the ranching life made their isolated existence the only one they would care to have. She saw the huge pens where the heifers awaited their first-born calves, and the pens where those who had already delivered took care of their long-legged youngsters until Jacob was sure they were ready to rejoin the rest of the herd. The older cows, she learned, calved out on the winter range, which was why a large blizzard was so devastating.

'I wish I'd seen a calf born,' she said to Clay, as, with evening drawing near, they left the camp. 'Could we come back again and stay longer some time?'

'As soon as it warms up, we'll ride on down and stay overnight with the Johnsons. That'll give you a chance to learn to ride at something faster than a walk. Sound good?' Clay cocked a quizzical eyebrow at Jennifer. She could tell he was challenging her to complain about the idea of riding so fast and so far.

'Lovely,' she replied, determined not to rise to the bait and send that know-it-all gleam into his eyes. 'Of course, I'll soon have legs shaped like a wishbone. They feel like it already, after this morning.'

'Always did like bow-legged girls,' Clay drawled, and then laughed as Jennifer shot him a black look. 'Now, Jenny, you're not going to get bow-legged from riding. I wouldn't let you on a horse if I thought it would spoil what I'm sure is a very pretty pair of legs. One of these days, I'm going to have a party so you'll put on a skirt.'

'I had one on when I arrived,' Jennifer said. 'I wore suits and high heels to work for years, but Clarence and Pam both told me I looked out of place on a ranch. I think I'd already feel that way myself.'

'As I said, a fast learner. Tell me about Chicago, aside from that Alan jerk. All you said on your application was that you wanted a change of scenery. Was that because of him?'

'Not entirely,' Jennifer said with a sigh. She told Clay about her quarrelsome family, and how tired she was of her futile efforts to be the peacemaker. 'I thought it was just my family, but it doesn't sound as if you and your brother get along any better,' she concluded, just as they turned through the gate at the drive to Clay's house. 'Why is it that relatives just can't get along?'

'Beats me,' Clay replied. 'Forrey and I got along fine when we were kids. Then we got into the college rodeo competition. I beat him at calf roping and bull riding and bronco riding. And I was a good student, too. I guess maybe he's resented that ever since, and figures the way to get even is to make me look like a crude country hick in comparison to him. I don't pay much attention to that. Hell, I like being a country hick.'

'A crude country hick that plays Mozart almost like a professional?' Jennifer teased. 'That doesn't fit very well.'

Clay shrugged. 'Forrey hates the fact that I can play, too. My mother was a music teacher and taught us both, but Forrey wouldn't practise. The only thing he ever got really good at was the bull whip. Maybe he thought he'd use it on me some day.' He looked over at Jennifer. 'I don't mind him pretending he's better than I am, and putting me down every chance that he gets, but I didn't want him meeting you right off and giving you the idea that I'm the family dunce. That's why I told him you were coming today instead of yesterday. So you could meet me first.' He grinned. 'Of course, you might have decided by now that I'm exactly what Forrest says without his help.'

'No chance,' Jennifer said, so quickly that Clay gave her a dazzling smile and squeezed her hand.

'Hey, that sounds good,' he said.

'Don't let it go to your head,' she replied, feeling her cheeks grow warm. 'Did what you said mean that Forrest is apt to be here tonight?'

'I'd say it was a sure thing,' Clay replied, as they rounded the row of pines. 'He was thick as thieves with old McDonald. Had a friend of his picked to replace him until I said no. I expect he'll probably want to check you out . . . well, speak of the devil,' he said with a chuckle. 'There's old Forrey's car. Brace yourself. You are about to meet the Cooper family version of Sir Galahad.'

'I can hardly wait,' Jennifer said sarcastically, eyeing Forrest Cooper's red Mercedes with distaste. 'He even drives the same kind of car that Alan did, except it's a lot newer and shinier.'

'He just bought it a couple of months ago. Paid cash for it, too. He claims he won the money at Vegas,' Clay said, with a sceptical lift of his eyebrows.

Jennifer frowned. 'You don't believe him?'

'That's an awful lot of luck,' Clay replied. He started to get out of the truck, but Jennifer stopped him.

'Clay,' she said, 'are you trying to tell me something?'

Clay looked at Jennifer intently for a moment, and then smiled. 'No,' he said, 'just reporting an interesting fact.'

Very interesting, Jennifer thought, as she followed Clay into the house. Clay's brother was paying cash for a Mercedes while Clay drove a middle-aged pick-up truck and cut back on other purchases. Somehow she would have to find out how he managed that. Of course, the brothers probably had separate finances too, but . . .

Forrest Cooper was not in the kitchen when they entered. It was probably beneath him, Jennifer thought, to sit and converse with the group of cowhands who had gathered for dinner. However, as soon as he heard Clay shout, 'Hey, Forrey, where in hell are you?' he came walking in from the living-room, carrying a glass of wine.

'Right here, brother dear. You don't need to yell,' he replied. His eyes fell on Jennifer and he smiled, a slow, seductive smile. 'Well, well. So this is the beautiful lady I've been hearing so much about.' He held out his hand. 'Miss Jennifer Tarkinton, I presume?'

Jennifer stared at him, momentarily speechless. If Clayton Cooper was handsome, Forrest Cooper was absolutely spectacular!

CHAPTER FOUR

JENNIFER could feel Clay's eyes on her as she stared at his brother. She glanced over at Clay and saw a look of watchful waiting on his face, as if he was wondering whether she was about to fall under Forrest's spell. Not on your life, she thought, quickly regaining her equilibrium. She lifted her chin and gave Forrest Cooper a pleasant but cool smile.

'That's right,' she said, taking the hand he offered in a brief handshake. 'You must be Forrest Cooper. Clay's told me a lot about you.'

'All of it bad, I assume,' Forrest said, giving Clay a cynical look. 'He can't stand the idea that I can do anything even reasonably well.'

'Not at all,' Jennifer replied, her years of practice with her bickering family leading her instinctively to disarm any potential argument. 'I understand that you're a super salesman who can practically charm the birds from the trees.'

Forrest stared at Jennifer blankly. 'He didn't,' he said.

Clay's eyes took on a devilish twinkle. 'I don't think Jenny would lie,' he said.

'Well, no, of course not,' Forrest said quickly. He raised his eyebrows and looked from Clay to Jennifer. 'I guess there's a first time for everything. But I'm sure that's not all that he told you.'

'That's all I can remember,' Jennifer said, and saw Clay struggling to keep from laughing out loud.

'You're going to have to get up pretty early to stay

ahead of this little lady,' he said.

'So I see,' Forrest said drily.

'Dinner's ready,' Nell called. 'Are you staying, Forrest? I set a place for you.'

Forrest looked for a moment as if he were about to refuse. Then he glanced at Jenny. 'Thank you,' was all that he said. Then he smiled at Jenny and took her arm.'Why don't you sit by me? I'd be interested in finding out exactly what Clay has been telling you since yesterday. You do know that he deliberately told me you wouldn't be here until today so that he could see you first, don't you? He didn't want you to have a chance to meet us together and make your own judgement.'

Jennifer gave him an innocent stare as she took the chair he held out for her. 'Are you sure? Maybe he just got the date wrong. Nell says that he seldom gets to meals on time.'

'He's really got you toeing the mark, hasn't he?' Forrest said, shaking his head as he sat down beside her. He looked past Jennifer to Clay, who sat at the head of the table. 'You know, if you just had a little class, you wouldn't have to be so worried about whether a female would give you a second look if she had a choice between us. I'm surprised you didn't have a posse waiting to keep me from coming here tonight. One day's hardly enough for you to get everything locked up.'

Clay put on an exaggeratedly hurt look. 'Jenny,' he said, 'what's this guy talking about? Have I been trying to do anything but show you what the ranching business is all about?'

Jennifer looked from Clay to Forrest and back again and frowned. Here she was, right in the middle of two warring relatives again, each trying to enlist her on his side. Well, she was going to put a stop to that, right now.

'Of course you have,' she said to Clay, whose face
went from smiling smugly to looking as if he had been
struck in an instant. Before Forrest could comment, she
turned to him. 'And I'm sure you'd have done the same
if you'd had the chance, so don't look so self-righteous.
Now there's something both of you should know. I am
here as an accountant, not as someone's potential
conquest.' She frowned at Forrest. 'You are already
married,' she said, then turned to Clay, 'and you are my
employer, so you can both forget anything else you had
in mind. Furthermore . . .' she took a deep breath '. . . I
listened to my parents arguing all of my life, until I
couldn't stand it any more and I am certainly not going
to listen to you two. If you can't get along when I'm
around and stop acting like I'm some kind of a prize
you're fighting over, then I . . . I quit!'

There was a murmur of approval among the
cowhands. Jennifer suddenly realised that perhaps she
should not have got so carried away in front of them and
looked down, embarrassed. She was surprised to hear
Forrest say, 'Fair enough, Jennifer. I apologise.' When
Clay said nothing, she looked at him. Her heart sank.
He looked both angry and unhappy. Oh, dear. She could
tell that he thought her outburst meant she had been
bowled over by Forrest's suave handsomeness, but she
hadn't. It was also obvious that, in spite of what he had
said earlier, Clay really did mind the comparison
between Forrest's elegance and his own more rugged
appearance. When he said nothing after she had looked
at him for several moments, she looked away again,
feeling depressed. Darn it all, she hadn't wanted to hurt
him. He was so gentle and kind. But she wasn't sure that
Forrest was quite the monster he had been painted,
either. They both seemed overly sensitive to their

differences. If only she could get them to accept each other for what they were. But she'd had no luck at that with her own family.

Jennifer sighed heavily and poked at the food on her plate. There was no way that she could eat anything now. She felt too miserable. She pushed her chair back from the table.

'Please excuse me. I'm not hungry,' she said, without meeting Clay's eyes. As she went through the door towards the stairs she heard Clarence growling, 'Now see what you two idiots have done? You made that nice little lady feel real bad.' That was a switch, she thought wryly. The first time Clarence had seen her, he hadn't liked her; now he was her defender.

Back in her room, Jennifer flipped on the television set and sat down in the lounge chair. She felt desperately in need of something to distract her. Deep inside, there was a terrible, aching feeling. Clay's hurt look haunted her. Well, what did he expect? Couldn't she even try to be fair, and give Forrest a chance? It wasn't as if she'd taken Forrest's side against him, although she could see why he might feel that she had. Damn! It would have been better if she'd just walked out without saying a word. Pretended she was sick. But something like this would probably have happened sooner or later, anyway.

After watching several sitcoms which did not give her a single laugh, Jennifer turned off the television and the lights in her room and stared out of the window at the starry night. Even without a moon, the snow gave a reflected soft lightness to the valley. It was such a beautiful place, so peaceful. Why couldn't people get along in a place like this? It made no sense at all. She turned away from the window, then turned quickly back at the sound of someone on the balcony. She pressed her face to the window and saw Clay at the far end, leaning against the railing and gazing off into the distance. He looked so alone. Maybe she should try harder to make him understand. Impulsively, she opened her balcony door and went towards him.

When Clay did not even look in her direction, Jennifer felt as if her heart would break. He doesn't even want to talk to me, she though unhappily. Nevertheless, she stopped beside him.

'It's a beautiful night,' she said softly, hoping for some response.

'Not especially,' he replied, without looking at her.

A lump lodged in Jennifer's throat. Somehow, she had to make Clay understand that she was not taking Forrest's side against him. 'Look, Clay,' she said, 'I realise that you got the impression that I let you down, but it wasn't——'

'Just drop it,' he said gruffly. 'I know what you were thinking.'

'You do not!' Jennifer cried, tears welling in her eyes. 'I am not taking Forrest's side against you. Just because I wouldn't——'

'I said drop it!' Clay said, giving Jennifer an angry glance. 'I was a fool to expect anything except what happened.'

'Oh, for heaven's sake, Clay, don't play the martyr,' Jennifer said, now feeling exasperated. 'You remind me of my mother.'

Clay stared into the distance again, his jaw set. 'I seem to remember,' he said finally, 'that that drove you away from home. Are you planning to leave here, too?'

'N-not unless you want me to,' Jennifer replied shakily. 'Do you?' She held her breath while she waited for Clay's answer. At last he turned and looked at her, his expression inscrutable in the dim light.

'No, I don't want you to go,' he said, after what seemed to Jennifer like an eternity. 'I need a good accountant. We'll see how you do at that, starting tomorrow. However, Forrey tells me that our father wants to meet you, so first thing in the morning we'll go over there. Wear a dress. My father's old-fashioned. He doesn't like women wearing jeans.'

Jennifer nodded. 'All right,' she said, although she felt far from all right herself. Clay had withdrawn from her so completely, he was so different from his previously warm, friendly self, that she could hardly tell he was the same person. When he said nothing more she said a quick goodnight and went back into her room. Once inside, she flung herself on her bed, buried her face in her pillows, and let out a scream of frustration. Why, oh, why, if she wasn't going to go along with Clay, hadn't she just kept her mouth shut?

In the morning, Jennifer took special care with her appearance, trying to cover the dark smudges under her eyes with make-up. She had lain awake for a long time, finally able to sleep when she'd rationalised that she probably couldn't have done anything differently. Too many years of getting caught in her own family's quarrelling had taken their toll.

'Try and remember to think before you speak today,' she reminded herself, as she surveyed the final results of her efforts in the mirror. She had chosen a bright printed challis dress, her favourite, in the hope that it would help hide the fact that she did not look too perky herself. Maybe, she thought hopefully, it would even get Clay out of his dark mood.

She heard him playing the piano when she went

downstairs and was tempted to go in and see him, but decided against it. She needed some coffee before she faced him again, just in case he was still as glum and withdrawn as he had been last night.

'Boy, do you look pretty,' Pam greeted her. 'I like that dress.'

'Thank you,' Jennifer said with a smile. At least Pam hadn't changed. 'I'm going to meet Mr Matt Cooper this morning. Sort of a command performance, I guess.'

Pam nodded. 'He's kind of a Grinch, but he's funny, too. He can make all kinds of animal noises, like a horse whinnying or a cow mooing. Sounds just like the real ones.' She got up suddenly and came to Jennifer's side. 'Is Uncle Clay still mad at you?' she whispered in her ear.

'I don't know. I haven't seen him this morning,' Jennifer replied. 'Did he tell you that he was mad at me?' She knew Pam had been at the table last night, but wasn't sure exactly how the little girl would have interpreted what had happened.

'No, but I could tell,' Pam replied. 'He kind of looks like he's going to explode, but he doesn't say anything. Sometimes he yells at Clarence and the cowhands, but he doesn't ever yell at me, and I don't think he will at you, either. He sure can yell at his brother, though. You should have heard him last night after you left. They went outside, but I could still hear.'

'Maybe you shouldn't tell me,' Jennifer said weakly. 'It's a private family quarrel.' She definitely did not want to hear that the brothers had continued their fighting.

Pam looked thoughtful, then made a face. 'It wasn't very private, because it was about you. Uncle Clay told Forrest he wished he'd go away and never come back, because he'd ruined everything with you. Then Forrest said he would come back, a lot, because he thought you were someone he could talk to. Uncle Clay said if he did, he'd shoot him. Then Forrest said that Uncle Clay ought to take lessons from him, instead, because his stra . . . strategy was all wrong, but if he was going to be shot at, he'd come armed.'

'Oh, Pam,' Jennifer said, horrified, 'I can't let that kind of thing go on. Maybe I'd better leave before there is some real bloodshed.'

'They don't really mean it,' Pam said quickly. 'I've heard them say stuff like that before. I think they're pretending this is still the Wild West. Besides, you can't go. I think Uncle Clay would really shoot his brother if you did.'

'He would?' Jennifer frowned. 'Why?'

'Because . . . Uh-oh, he's coming.' Pam put her lips next to Jennifer's ear. 'Because he's in love with you,' she whispered. She giggled at Jennifer's startled expression and danced back to her chair. 'Hi, Uncle Clay,' she said with an ingenuous smile. 'You weren't playing very well this morning.'

'Just what we need around here,' Clay said, giving Pam a mock disgusted look. 'A ten-year-old music critic.' He looked down at Jennifer as he took his seat. 'You look very nice this morning,' he said formally.

'Thank you. So do you,' Jennifer replied with equal formality, trying to ignore the sag of disappointment that hit her especially hard after the brief flurry of hope that Pam's confidence had caused.

Clay was wearing a dark grey western-style suit with a white western shirt and a bolo tie with a huge turquoise and silver thunderbird. Did his father demand that he get dressed up, she wondered, or was he taking Forrest's hint that he should change his strategy? He did not look especially angry this morning, but neither did he look very relaxed. Uptight, she decided, was the word that would best describe his appearance. He responded good-naturedly enough to the cowhands' comments on his appearance, his excuse for it being that he didn't want 'Jennifer' to have to go visiting with someone in jeans, when she was so well dressed. He made no comment on her scanty breakfast. And, when they went outside for their drive to Matt Cooper's house, he gestured to the waiting car rather stiffly.

'I didn't want you to think I had no decent car of my own to drive,' he said.

'Decent car? It's beautiful!' Jennifer exclaimed, staring at the beautifully restored bright red Thunderbird sports car. 'I think this was one of the prettiest cars ever made.' She got into the luxurious white leather seat and looked around delightedly. 'I've never been in one of these, but I've always wanted to.'

'I'm glad you like it. Restoring cars is my hobby. I also have an old, but very elegant, Cadillac limousine.'

Good lord, he doesn't even sound like himself, Jennifer thought, glancing at his chiselled profile and then biting her lip. Should she tell him to cut it out, or just let this aberration run its course? He surely wouldn't keep up this act for too long? He knew what she thought of dull, pompous men like Alan. Of course, there was still the possibility that it wasn't an act. Maybe he was just covering up the fact that he was still angry with her by becoming unbearably formal.

Clay said nothing except a rather stilted comment on what a terrible mess the melting snow made of his clean car as they drove the short distance to his father's house. When they stopped in front of the huge old ranch house with its long porch across the front, he quickly got out and opened the car door for Jennifer.

'I do hope you won't find my father too blunt,' he said, as he offered her his arm. 'He has a tendency to say what he thinks without embellishment.'

'I'm looking forward to meeting him,' Jennifer replied, fighting to keep a straight face. The whole situation was beginning to strike her as hysterically funny, and she was terribly afraid she might have another attack of the giggles.

'Good morning, Mrs Young,' Clay said when the housekeeper answered the door. 'This is Jennifer Tarkinton. Is my father prepared to meet her?'

The housekeeper gave Clay a strange look. 'Glad to meet you, Miss Tarkinton. Of course he's ready to see you. Go right on in. I'll bring some coffee.'

Clay escorted Jennifer down a long hall to a large room at the end of the house, where a hospital bed had been placed in what had once been a sitting-room, with huge windows looking out at the valley on either side of a stone fireplace. The moment she laid eyes on the man propped up in the bed, Jennifer knew she would have recognised him anywhere as Clay's father. The thick thatch of hair was now white, but the blue eyes were as bright, and the face was permanently tanned from his years as a rancher.

Before Clay could even speak, the old man thundered, 'What's got you so dressed up today, Clayton? Going to a funeral? I'm not ready to die just yet.'

At that Jennifer did laugh out loud. Clay looked uncomfortable, but his father grinned delightedly.

'Well, just look at that pretty little critter that fancy-pants son of mine brought to see me,' Matt

Cooper said, holding his hand out towards Jennifer. 'Come on over here and let me get a good look at you.' He took her hand in a firm grip. 'Bend over and give me a kiss, girl,' he said. 'I don't get much of that stuff any more.'

'You need to put your bed in a better location,' she teased, smiling into his twinkling blue eyes after giving his cheek a kiss. 'I don't think you'd have any trouble getting a lot of kisses.'

'By golly, you've got an idea there,' Matt Cooper said, grinning and scratching his head. 'Where do you think I ought to put it?'

'Maybe a shopping mall?' Jennifer suggested.

Matt Cooper roared with laughter and patted Jennifer's hand. 'That's a good one,' he said. 'A real good one. So you're the lady accountant. Jennifer. Jenny. How'd such a pretty lady get into that business? Always sounded awfully dull to me.'

For a while, Jennifer and Matt talked, first about her job and then about the Bar-C Ranch. Within half an hour, Jennifer felt as if she were talking to an old and dear friend. Clay sat in a chair, drinking his coffee and speaking only when spoken to. At last his father frowned at him.

'You're about as quiet as I've ever seen you, boy,' he said. 'What's the matter? The cat got your tongue?'

Clay shook his head. 'No. I thought you were handling the conversational end of things quite well by yourself.'

That remark, Jennifer noticed, brought forth a look from Matt very similar to the one Mrs Young had given Clay.

'I guess that's right,' he said. 'Well, while you're so nice and quiet, I might as well ask you something very

important.' He reached out and took Jennifer's hand in
his and patted it again. 'When are you going to ask Jenny
to marry you? This here's the gal for you, Clayton. I can
tell.'

Clay almost choked on his coffee. 'I think it's a little
soon, Father,' he said when he had stopped coughing.
'She just got here the day before yesterday.'

'Nonsense,' Matt said positively. 'Either you know
or you don't. Isn't that right, Jenny?'

Jennifer swallowed. Clay was watching her intently.
Think first, she reminded herself. 'I—er—guess in
some cases that's true,' she replied, 'but I don't think it
always works that way.'

'Well, see that it does work, one way or another,' Matt
told her firmly. 'You need a husband and Clayton needs
a wife. Time's a-wasting. I want to be at the wedding.'

Jennifer cast a desperate glance in Clay's direction.
He was obviously going to be no help. For the first time
that day he looked as if he was enjoying himself. She
tried giving Matt a whimsical smile. 'I'll think about it,'
she said, 'but I heard a song the other day called "Never
Marry a Cowboy". It sounded like they're a pretty hard
group to live with.'

'Why, we make the best husbands there are,' Matt
said. 'Isn't that right, Clayton?'

'If you don't count Forrest,' Clay replied quietly.

'I don't,' Matt said with his usual firmness. 'He's not
a real cowboy. Never had his heart in it. Lord knows
I've tried, but it's like trying to turn a racehorse into a
plough horse.' He frowned as a starched looking woman
in a nurse's uniform appeared in the doorway. 'Oh, no.
Not time for my medicine already, is it?'

'I'm afraid so,' the nurse replied.

'I don't need any when there's a pretty girl to look

at,' Matt grumbled. 'Makes the old ticker work just
fine.' He squeezed Jennifer's hand. 'I'll probably have
to take a nap now, too. You come back and see me again
soon, you hear?'

'I will,' Jennifer promised. Impulsively, she bent and
kissed Matt firmly on the lips.

'Well, how about that?' he said, grinning happily.
'Maybe I ought to marry you myself.'

'That's an offer I'd seriously consider,' Jennifer
replied with a smile.

'You certainly made a good impression on my father,'
Clay said, when they were back in his car.

'He made a big hit with me,' Jennifer said. 'He's a
darling. I think I really could fall in love with him.
What's wrong with him, Clay? Is it his heart?'

Clay nodded. 'Congestive heart failure. He won't be
around too much longer, I'm afraid.'

'How sad.' Jennifer had a lump in her throat as she
looked across the valley, where Matt Cooper and his
father before him had built the Bar-C Ranch with years
of dedicated labour that had triumphed over hard times
and disasters. Now it was Clay's and Forrest's, but, so
far, there were no grandchildren to carry on after them.
No wonder Matt was so eager for Clay to marry. She
glanced thoughtfully at Clay. He would be a wonderful
father. The way he took care of Pam showed that. And
the Clay she had met when she'd first arrived was a
wonderful man, so warm and loving. It had been a bit
of a shock to her at first, but she knew now that she liked
him that way. This new, Forrest-type disguise was far
less appealing. Once again, she wondered if she should
simply tell him to stop it, but again she held back. If only
she knew exactly why he was doing it!

They arrived back at Clay's house in time for lunch.

'Will wonders never cease?' Nell commented. 'Of course, I don't know if we're fancy enough for you two. We're just having chilli dogs and coleslaw.'

'That sounds terrific,' Jennifer said. 'I'm going to run upstairs and change before I eat. I'm tired of being so fancy.' And just maybe, she thought hopefully, Clay will stop acting so stiff and formal if he puts on his regular clothes too. Her hopes were dashed as soon as she returned to the table. He had not changed his clothes. He had taken off his jacket and unbuttoned his collar, but he still looked as stoic as ever, a newspaper held up in front of him like a shield. 'I assume you plan to show me the office after lunch,' she said, trying to start a conversation.

'I certainly do,' he replied. He folded his newspaper and devoured his lunch silently, while Jennifer toyed briefly with the idea of throwing a bowl of chilli at him, and then discarded it. Clay might get hurt, and she wouldn't want that. Too bad she hadn't tried it on Alan, though. He would have looked wonderful with beans dripping down his face. She smiled to herself at the thought. She caught Clay watching her and smiled at him.

'I haven't seen you smile today,' she said. 'Are you ill?'

He shook his head, but did not smile. 'No. Just thinking about some serious matters,' he replied. 'Are you ready to see the office?'

'I've been ready since I arrived,' Jennifer said coldly. Clay's charade was beginning to get on her nerves. If it was a charade. If it wasn't, he ought to have his head examined.

'Follow me,' Clay said, getting up from the table. 'I only have one key to the office. I'll have another made for you.'

'Have one made for yourself!' Jennifer snapped. 'I'm the one who'll be using the office. In fact,' she added, as they stopped in front of the door, 'you can give me the key right now.'

Clay shrugged. 'Suit yourself.' He handed the key to Jennifer. 'Here you are.'

Jennifer inserted the key and opened the door. She looked into the room, took one step forwards, and then stopped. 'Good lord,' she said, looking up at Clay in horror. 'What's happened in here? It looks like a tornado went through it!'

CHAPTER FIVE

FOR the first time that day, Clay momentarily looked as if he were about to break into his wide, boyish grin. Instead, he quickly controlled it. 'It is rather a mess, isn't it?' he said calmly.

'A mess? It looks as if your last accountant were a chimpanzee!' Jennifer exclaimed, her eyes sweeping from one disorderly pile of papers to another. There were two steel desks in the room, their tops littered as if someone had emptied a rubbish basket on to them. The file drawers hung open, folders sticking out at odd angles and preventing them from closing. One desk in the far corner, which held a computer, looked reasonably tidy.

'It's not his fault. I was looking for something one day after he left,' Clay said calmly. 'There didn't seem much point in putting things back, since I couldn't remember where things went, anyway. It would only have made it worse.'

'How thoughtful of you!' Jennifer snapped, glaring at him. 'Now I can see why you kept this place locked, and why you wanted to hire someone from far away who wouldn't know what they were getting into. I should have suspected something when Clarence said you didn't like this part of ranching. But why on earth didn't someone else try to straighten it up? Tanya, for instance?'

'Because I told her not to. She's been keeping the records current on the computer, paying the bills, and meeting the payroll. All the rest of this . . .' he made a sweeping gesture with his hand '. . . is the records of the past year. You can go over it as you put it in order.'

'This is all of the records?' Jennifer asked.

'Well, no.' Clay frowned. 'I think there are still quite a few files, but they weren't relevant to what I was looking for.'

'And exactly what was it you were trying to find?' Jennifer asked resignedly. It was becoming obvious that Clayton Cooper was one of those people for whom the intricacies of financial organisation and record-keeping were a complete mystery.

'I was trying to find out why we weren't showing more of a profit. From the number of cattle I shipped at the prices we were supposed to have received, it didn't seem right. It still doesn't.'

'Why,' Jennifer asked patiently, 'didn't you ask the man—McDonald, wasn't it?—to show you? I'm sure he could have made it clear.' Even to a mathematical moron, she thought uncharitably.

'I did. He said he'd try to pull everything together so that it would be clear, but before he could do it his mother in California had a stroke, and he had to leave suddenly.'

If only he had waited for her to get here, Jennifer thought with a sigh. 'How long ago did Mr McDonald leave?' she asked.

'About three months ago,' Clay replied.

'Three months?' Jennifer cried. 'Has Tanya been keeping up with all of the IRS forms, too?'

'I'm not sure, but I think so,' Clay replied.

'I hope so,' Jennifer said fervently. She had visions of inquisitors from the Internal Revenue Service descending on the Bar-C, demanding to know why no withholding forms had been filed, no estimated taxes sent. She took a deep breath. 'Well . . .' she pulled her glasses from her bag and put them on '. . . I'd better plunge in somewhere. I'd like to have Tanya come here immediately. I might need even more help, but I'll wait and see.'

'I'm not sure whether I can get her here until tomorrow,' Clay said slowly. 'She lives in Bozeman, and she might be busy.'

'She hasn't seen busy yet,' Jennifer said coldly. 'I hope she's ready for a full-time job. And, unless you want me to just set fire to this entire mess, I suggest you try very hard to convince her to come today. I have hopes she can save me a lot of trouble. And one other thing,' she added, as Clay started to leave, 'don't you *ever* come in here without my permission. I'd as soon have Coal King come prancing through.'

'Yes, ma'am,' Clay replied, once again looking as if he were about to smile. This time, he quickly turned and walked away.

Jennifer shook her head and closed the door behind him. Clayton Cooper was definitely the strangest man she had ever met. How could anyone with his casual attitude towards record-keeping possibly run a huge, successful ranch? Or wasn't it as successful as it seemed? For all Clay knew, they might be on the verge of bankruptcy. Maybe Forrest was the one with some business sense, after all. She would have to have him come over and go over his end of the business some time soon. As soon as she knew enough to be able to ask him some intelligent questions.

Clay brought Tanya to the office by late afternoon. She was a small, delicate-looking woman with long brown hair, not at all the glamorous creature Jennifer had expected Forrest's wife would be.

'I can stay as long as you want,' she told Jennifer, with a shy smile. 'It'll be nice to be busy again.'

'We'll be busy, all right,' Jennifer replied. 'I'm going to set up a whole new system. From what I've seen, I don't like Mr McDonald's system at all.'

'I never did, either,' Tanya said, 'but he didn't take suggestions very well. Do you want to work a while after dinner?'

'If you don't mind, I think we should,' Jennifer said. 'Mr Cooper has succeeded in getting things so disorganised that it might be a week before we can start making any real progress.' She gave Clay, who was standing silently, listening to the two women, a meaningful lift of her eyebrows.

Clay made a brief deferential bow towards Jennifer and Tanya. 'I'm, sure that you two talented ladies will be able to restore order to this office in record time,' he said, 'so I will leave you to it. if I can be of any assistance, don't hesitate to call on me. Dinner will be at six.'

After he had left, Tanya turned to Jennifer, frowning. 'Clay's acting very strange,' she said. 'Usually he dresses like a cowhand and acts more like a big, friendly puppy dog. Has he been like this all the time since you got here?'

Jennifer shook her head. 'He was a nice, friendly cowboy when I got here. This overly formal business just started this morning. I have no idea what he thinks he's accomplishing with it. It may have something to do with——' She stopped herself and shrugged. It probably wouldn't be wise to discuss with Tanya Clay's fight with Forrest, in view of the problem that had driven her away.

'That's OK,' Tanya said. 'I heard about the fight he

and Forrest had last night. Word gets around fast when the cowhands hit the bars. Everyone likes to hear the latest on the battling Cooper brothers.' She smiled. 'I also heard that Clay's really sweet on you. I thought that might be why he's so dressed up.'

'Oh, dear,' Jennifer groaned. 'It's like living in a fish bowl. Well, I'm not sweet on anybody, but I was definitely much more impressed with Clay when I first got here. Especially before I saw this mess! Shall we see if we can make a start? I need a few bits of information you may have, and I haven't dared to turn on the computer yet. Can you show me what's on it?'

'Oh, sure,' Tanya said quickly. 'That's one thing I do know about. Mr McDonald was kind of old-fashioned. He was practically computer-phobic, so he left me pretty much alone when I used it. The trouble is, he wouldn't give me everything, so some things are incomplete.'

'Let's hope the rest is here somewhere,' Jennifer said grimly, 'or this might be like an archaeological expedition, trying to reconstruct a whole civilisation from bits and pieces.'

For the rest of that afternoon and evening, and every day and night thereafter for the next week, Jennifer worked diligently on bringing order out of the chaos, trying to ignore the fact that Clay remained distant and coolly formal with her. It was clear that he was acting out some kind of charade for her benefit, for in the morning he would leave, dressed in his cowboy apparel, apparently carrying on his normal life during the day. Then he would return in time to get dressed in a suit before dinner, and carry on a stilted conversation about world affairs or the sorry state of the farm economy.

'If I weren't so busy, I'd be miserable,' she said one

day, having finally confided in Tanya the details of her misguided attempt to stop the brothers' fighting that ill-fated night. 'I really did like Clay so much the way he was, and he seemed to like me, too. I'd think he was trying to be suave and sophisticated like Forrest in the hopes that it would impress me, except that he knows I don't go for that type of man. Can he be trying to push me by reminding me of someone I don't like simply because he decided that he doesn't like me after all? I didn't think he'd do anything like that.'

'He wouldn't,' Tanya said quickly. 'He's one of the kindest, gentlest men I know. And I'm sure he does like you. When you're not looking he watches you as if he could hardly tear his eyes away.' She frowned thoughtfully. 'Forrest didn't act like he does now before we were married. When I first met him, back in college, he was much more like Clay. Then, when his father told him he wouldn't inherit anything from him if he went off to become a jazz pianist like he wanted to, he started to change. I told him I didn't care about the money, but he's determined that Clay isn't going to get everything the Coopers own, so he keeps hanging on, doing something he hates, and acting like a complete fool most of the time. I'd give anything if he'd just move out and do what he wants. That's why I won't divorce him. I still love him and hope that eventually he'll come to his senses. Of course, once his father dies, and he has his share of the ranch, I don't know what he'll do. Maybe he and Clay will finally have that shoot-out they've been threatening to have for years.'

'Oh, Tanya, we can't let that happen,' Jennifer said, her heart going out to the unhappy little woman. 'There must be something that could bring all three of them together, Clay and Forrest, and their father.'

'A grandchild might have helped,' Tanya said sadly, 'but I had trouble getting pregnant and then I miscarried. Forrest was so disappointed. It was after that that he started wearing really fancy clothes and running around.'

'Hmm,' Jennifer said, frowning. 'If I remember my psychology right, that sounds like some kind of a defence mechanism. I'll have to think about that for a while. Meanwhile, we'd better get back to work.'

Tanya, Jennifer had discovered, had a good instinct for organisation, and an excellent memory, which enabled them to find things that Mr McDonald had buried in obscure files.

'He liked to put everything to do with one operation together,' Tanya said, when Jennifer asked her why a new pasture gate and a new roof on a barn at the Johnsons' appeared on the same list as medicinal supplies. 'The trouble is, he sometimes forgot to put things like gates and roofs on the depreciation schedule. I tried to catch them, but I wasn't always quick enough.'

'I thought we might need a complete inventory the first day when Clay showed me round,' Jennifer said with a sigh. 'I think I'll put you in charge of that, and we'll ask Clay to assign one of the men to help out. I hope he can spare someone now.'

'Certainly,' Clay said, when she approached him the next morning at breakfast. 'I'll ask Barkley to assist you. Since he's our roving handyman, he's familiar with almost everything.'

'Thank you,' Jennifer said, giving him her warmest smile, in the hope that it might thaw some of the ice. 'I'd really appreciate that. I also wanted to tell you that we're making good progress, and I might have something to show you in another week.'

'Good,' Clay replied, smiling briefly. 'I'm looking forward to seeing what you've done.'

'There is one other thing,' Jennifer went on, still smiling sweetly. 'I was wondering how you know exactly how many cattle you've shipped each year. I've got the totals that Forrest turned in to Mr McDonald, but there's no other record that I can find.'

Clay cleared his throat. 'Well, we count them when they're cut into the shipping pens, and again when they're loaded into the trucks. I have a record of that in my room. If you like, I'll get it for you.'

'Please do,' Jennifer said. 'I think it should be part of our permanent records, don't you?'

'By all means,' Clay agreed. He excused himself and returned a few minutes later with a large notebook. 'I hope you'll be able to decipher this without too much trouble,' he said, as he handed it to Jennifer.

'Decipher it?' Jennifer asked, raising her eyebrows at Clay. She opened the book, expecting the worst. Instead, the pages were neatly labelled and the writing was clear and precise. In addition to the numbers, there were descriptions of each load, the weight of each load of animals, the name of the driver and his destination. 'Why, Clay, this is very good!' Jennifer exclaimed, smiling at him. 'It's just what I was looking for.'

For an instant, Jennifer could have sworn she saw a twinkle of mischief in Clay's eyes, but he looked away so quickly that she could not be sure.

'I'm glad you approve,' he said, staring out of the window at the end of the room. 'Lovely day,' he remarked. 'Spring is definitely upon us. I hope you're taking some time to get outside in the fresh air. All work and no play, and all that.'

'I haven't had time,' Jennifer said with a sigh. 'Maybe

in another week or so I'll be able to.'

Clay shook his head. 'Spring passes all too quickly,' he said, still gazing into the distance. 'Tomorrow we should take the promised ride to the Johnsons'. It's been far too long since you were on horseback. We'll stay overnight and come back the following morning.'

'I'm sorry, Clay, but I really don't feel I should take the time right now,' Jennifer said, thinking unhappily that, as far as the horseback riding was concerned, it hadn't been long enough, but if the old Clay were to ask her she'd jump at the chance to spend the day with him. It was beginning to feel like a lifetime ago when he had kissed her and made her laugh, an experience that seemed more wonderful in retrospect with each day of drudgery and neglect from Clay.

'Then I'll have to order you to go,' Clay said, turning his head back to look at her, the now all-too-familiar inscrutable expression firmly in place. 'If you want to keep your job, you will accompany me to the Johnsons' tomorrow.'

Jennifer stared at him, unable to believe her ears. 'Of all the nerve——' she began, and then stopped. Something funny was going on here. Suddenly there was a deep, intense fire in Clay's eyes instead of the blank stare she had had from him recently. Was there some chance that when they were off, alone together, he would explain why he had adopted his strange behaviour? Perhaps even revert to his former self? She bit her lip. Even if there was, she wasn't going to let him think he could threaten her like that. She didn't like it. 'Would you mind rephrasing your request?' she said icily. 'I don't respsond well to threats. I might very well quit rather than go with you under those conditions.'

This time, Jennifer was sure of the flash of devilment

that crossed Clay's face.

'Perhaps I was too harsh,' he said, one corner of his mouth twitching. 'I would appreciate it if you would reconsider and accompany me. It's sure to be a very pleasant experience, and one that will rejuvenate your body as well as your mind. You've seemed a little tired and peaked lately.'

'All right,' I'll go,' Jennifer said, her eyes narrowed as she studied Clay intently. Tomorrow, she vowed, she would see that it was a pleasant experience—or die trying. She would let him know exactly what she thought of his endless mimicking of someone entirely unlike his real, dynamic self.

For the rest of the day, she found it difficult to concentrate on her work, trying to rehearse in her mind the different ways she might tell Clay to go back to being the man she had first met. At first she thought it was her lack of concentration that led to an odd discrepancy in the cattle sales records. The total number shipped was the same from both Clay and Forrest, but any way she figured it the total receipts did not seem to match. Tanya had a printout of the amounts paid at the auctions on the days the cattle were taken in, and, unless the cattle weighed literally thousands of pounds less than Clay's figures suggested, there was something amiss.

'Could those figures be that far off?' she asked Tanya.

'I doubt it,' Tanya replied. 'Cattle often lose some weight during shipping due to stress, but nowhere near that much.'

'We'd better dig back through the bank deposit records and make sure McDonald didn't skip something,' Jennifer said. 'Maybe you can do that tomorrow while I go on my enforced rehabilitation trip.'

Tanya looked at Jennifer knowingly. 'I'll bet you're not nearly as reluctant to go as you sound. Besides, maybe if you get Clay alone you can find out what he's up to.'

'I'm planning on it,' Jennifer said.

In the morning, Jennifer was on tenterhooks with a combination of apprehension and excitement. Deep inside she had a feeling that something special was going to happen, although there was nothing she could put her finger on that would justify it. At breakfast, Pam brought her one of her own cowboy hats.

'You've got to have one to look like a real cowgirl,' she said, as she tried it on Jennifer's head. Jennifer's topknot was in the way. 'I'll fix it,' Pam said, removing the combs that held it and smoothing Jennifer's hair down before she could protest. 'There,' she said, putting the hat on Jennifer at a rakish angle. 'That looks terrific. With that denim jacket and your boots, no one would guess that you're really an accountant.'

'The horse will know,' Jennifer said drily. She took off the hat, shook her long hair back over her shoulders, and replaced the hat just as Clay came into the room. There was, she decided as she met his eyes, definitely something cooking behind them. They were positively smouldering with a controlled fire, even though his greeting was still formal.

'Good morning, Jennifer,' he said, as he took his place at the table. 'You look appropriately dressed for our trip.'

Pam made an unpleasant, snorting noise. 'Why don't you tell her she looks gorgeous?' she asked. 'I can tell that's what you're thinking.'

Clay cocked an eyebrow at Pam. 'Why don't you devote your mind-reading talents to figuring out what your teacher wants you to know for your geography test so you don't mess it up like you did the last one?'

'I already do know,' Pam said, lifting her chin defiantly. 'We've got to know all the countries of Europe and be able to write the names on a blank map. Could you do that?'

'I'm not sure I could,' Clay admitted. A lively discussion followed, with Pam opening her book to show everyone where such difficult countries as Bulgaria were located. Jennifer began to relax a little. Clay seemed so normal now, as he teased Pam and joked with the cowhands. Perhaps he'd stay that way when they left. But, when the time came for them to leave, he became formal once again.

'Well, Jennifer, shall we be off?' he asked. 'I do believe it's a perfect day for a ride.'

'Lovely,' Jennifer agreed, gritting her teeth. She dearly wished that Clay had said, 'Let's get moving, Jenny,' and then put his arm around her and hugged her. She was beginning to have an aching physical longing for his touch. Maybe, she thought glumly, she was just perverse. She hadn't appreciated it nearly so much when it was available.

Clay said nothing as they walked, side by side, to the stables, and made only minimal comments as they got Midnight and Ace from their stalls. Jennifer began to feel a growing irritation, but said nothing. In spite of her vow to tell Clay to snap out of his stuffy, stilted charade, she had not been able to decide exactly how and when to do so. 'Play it by ear,' Tanya had suggested, and she had agreed that she'd have to do just that.

'Do you still remember what you learned about saddling a horse?' Clay asked, when they had the horses ready to be saddled.

'Most of it,' Jennifer replied. 'But I'm not quite sure about tightening the girth strap. Could you show me that again?'

'I'd be happy to,' Clay said. He watched as Jennifer put on the saddle blanket, threw the saddle across Midnight's back, and pulled the girth across beneath her stomach. 'Very good, Jennifer,' he said. 'Now, if you'll stand aside, I'll show you how to tighten the girth.'

At Clay's words, all of Jennifer's frustrations seemed to congeal into a white ball of fury. Still clutching the strap, she looked at him, her eyes narrowed. 'Would you repeat that, please?' she spat out in loud, staccato tones. 'No, don't! Don't say another damned word to me if you're going to talk like that. "Very good, Jennifer," she mocked, in a stilted, high-pitched voice. '"Now, if you'll stand aside, I'll show you how to tighten the girth."' She glared at him, breathing hard. 'What is wrong with you? Why are you acting like such an idiot?'

Clay's eyes were twinkling, his mouth twisted into an amused smile. 'Have I been?' he asked.

'You know very well you have!' Jennifer shouted. 'And if you don't stop it, I'm not going anywhere with you, today or any other day!'

'OK, Jenny,' Clay said, his wide, boyish grin reappearing like spring sunshine. 'I think I've made my point.' He reached for the girth.

'Just a minute,' Jennifer said, her momentary pleasure at seeing Clay's smile suddenly disappearing in a new flash of anger. 'What point?' Are you trying to tell me that you had something in mind? It wasn't simply temporary insanity? You'd better explain yourself, or I'm still not going with you.'

'All right,' Clay replied with a shrug. 'I was damned upset when you pulled the rug out from under me in front of Forrest that night. In fact, I was madder than hell. So I thought I'd let you find out what it would be like if I was always polite and proper, and didn't expect anything from you but the same. I got the picture that you didn't like it quite a while ago, but I thought I'd hang in there until you said something about it. That way I'd really be sure you appreciated me for what I am.' He grinned as Jennifer continued to glare at him. 'Don't look so mad, Jenny, my girl,' he said. 'It was a good idea to back off for a while. I was getting a little ahead of myself, anyway.'

'I'm not mad, I'm furious!' Jennifer snapped. 'You paid no attention to the fact that *I* was upset at being stuck in the middle between you and Forrest. I knew you were hurt, and I felt sorry afterwards, but darn it, Clay, I've been in that position all my life and I won't be used like that any more. Either get that through your head right now or you can speak Russian for all I care. I won't listen to you.' She watched, still trembling with the aftermath of her anger, as Clay silently took the girth from her hand, then tucked her hand behind him and closed his arms around her.

'I'm sorry, Jenny,' he said, his eyes softly pleading as he looked into hers. 'Like I said, I got ahead of myself. I shouldn't have expected you to go along with me like that. It was too much to expect, too soon. Can you forgive me?'

'I guess so,' Jennifer replied, still troubled. 'But can't I please have a chance to even try to like Forrest? I'm not going to get swept off my feet by him. He's not my type. Besides, I know Tanya still loves him, and I like her a lot. I'd give anything if something could bring them together again. And you and Forrest, too.' She smiled wryly. 'I guess I'm still a peacemaker at heart.'

'There's nothing wrong with that,' Clay said, pulling her close. He took her hat off and set it on Midnight's back. 'I like your hair down,' he said softly, stroking it with his hand. His arms tightened around her and he laid his cheek against her hair. 'You're something special, Jenny,' he said. 'I like everything about you. But don't go getting your sweet little heart broken, trying to fix things that can't be fixed.'

Jennifer sighed, her head nestled against Clay's shoulder. 'I'll try not to,' she said.

She closed her eyes and let the remnants of her tension drain away, erased by the warmth of Clay's embrace. It wasn't quite the same this time, she thought, the feeling of his arms around her, the sensation of holding on to someone strong she got from closing her arms around him. It was still wonderful and exciting, but the shock was gone. She felt as if she belonged there. Could this be love, this warm, peaceful feeling? Pam had said Clay loved her, but he had only said that he liked her . . . Slow down, Jennifer, she told herself. Maybe you're the one who's getting ahead of herself now. She raised her head and looked at Clay. The peaceful feeling vanished in a surge of excitement that shook her to her toes. The look of intense, yearning hunger in Clay's eyes was unmistakable.

Clay smiled slowly, his eyes lingering on Jennifer's parted lips. She knew that he wanted to kiss her, and her pulse raced madly, but instead he took a deep breath and seemed to discipline himself. He smiled wryly and winked.

'Let's get moving, Jenny,' he said. 'Time's a-wasting.' He released her and quickly tightened the girth. 'Mount up,' he said.

Jennifer put her foot in the stirrup and swung into the

saddle. Clay chuckled and handed her the reins.

'You do that like an old hand,' he said. 'I was kind of surprised that you didn't complain about going for a long ride and getting bow-legged.'

'I've been too busy wondering what was wrong with you,' Jennifer said with a grimace. 'Now I'm wondering what was wrong with me that I didn't complain. I hope we're not going to gallop all of the way. Poor old Midnight might keel over.'

'We'll take it easy on both of you,' Clay said, as he swung into his saddle. 'OK, let's move 'em out. We'll go slow until we get out in the fields. Let you get used to the feel again.'

Jennifer nodded, trying to relax and feel the horse beneath her as she had before.

They followed the drive away from the ranch house until it crossed the bridge over the creek, which was running bank-full from the melted snow. Clay dismounted and let them through a gate into a pasture, now green and lush from the warmth of the sun.

'In the summer we can ford the creek,' Clay said, as they cut off across the huge expense. 'It's only a couple of feet deep then, most places, but still cold as ice. It's a great place to cool off your feet on a hot day. Makes 'em feel all tingly and good.' He looked over at Jennifer and grinned. 'OK, here we go. We'll canter a while. Just give Middie her head and she'll keep up.'

Clay urged Ace forward, and the big gelding broke into a slow, rocking canter. Midnight hesitated a moment, and then followed suit. Jennifer felt her tension return. She clutched at the pommel. Clay glanced at her and frowned.

'Let go,' he ordered firmly. 'Hold on with your thighs. That's it,' as Jennifer shakily complied. 'You aren't going to fall off unless you faint,' he said teasingly.

'That's what worries me,' she replied. Nevertheless, she managed to adjust herself well enough to the motion that she was soon enjoying the feeling of the soft spring air in her face and the sensation of moving swiftly across the ground. 'Why did we stop? I was doing just fine,' she complained, when, after about a quarter of a mile, Clay pulled his horse in.

'Lesson time,' Clay said, as he dismounted. 'Need to teach you a few tricks of the trade now that you've seen what it's like.' He gave Jennifer some pointers on how to sit, the right position for her legs and feet, and how to use the reins to get Midnight to change lead. 'We'll go further this time,' he said, as he remounted his horse, 'and then we'll walk a while so we can talk and look at the scenery. It's too pretty a day to rush through it.' He smiled. 'Besides, I wouldn't want my pretty little Jenny-wren to get all tired and cross and bow-legged.'

Jennifer smiled, but said nothing as they started off again. Her heart felt so buoyant at Clay's high spirits that she doubted anything could tire her today. Being with Clay in the world that he loved was like drinking from a fountain of energy, fed by an eternal spring of delight.

They slowed the horses after a while, and Clay told her of his days as a child, first learning to ride with the cowhands, then to do their work as a man when he was still but a boy.

'I thought I was really big the first time I roped a little calf and threw it,' he said with a grin. 'My daddy cut me down to size real fast. Got me a much bigger one to go after the next time, and laughed his head off when it got away from me.'

'I've never seen a rodeo, except on television,' Jennifer said.

'You'll see the part that real cowboys do when we have the round-up starting next month,' Clay replied. 'We'll get all of the new cattle branded and the whole herd moved to summer pasture in the mountains behind us. It takes about six weeks altogether, if everything goes smoothly. By the end, it's getting pretty hot, and it gets a little tiresome.'

'I can imagine,' Jennifer said. From her recent accounting work, she knew that over seven thousand calves had been branded at the Bar-C the previous year.

They alternately cantered and walked, the hills at the northeastern edge of the valley drawing swiftly nearer. They were cantering easily along when suddenly Jennifer waved her hand to signal Clay and pulled Midnight to a stop.

'Look over there,' she said, pointing towards the east. 'Are those some of your cattle?'

Clay shook his head. 'That's a herd of elk stopping by on their way to their summer haunts in the mountains.'

'How marvellous,' Jennifer said, smiling delightedly. 'I've never seen anything like that, just roaming around free.'

'They aren't free, they're eating my pasture,' Clay said with a grin. 'Some fence went down in the storm, and they're taking advantage of an easier route. It happens almost every year.'

'You don't seem to mind,' Jennifer commented.

'No, I like to see them,' Clay replied, 'as long as there aren't too many. We'll get the fence up and they'll be gone in a few days.'

They moved slowly towards the elk, their horses'

hoofs making only a soft, swishing noise through the grass. Jennifer soon saw that the elk were far bigger than cattle, their cream-coloured rumps shining like beacons in contrast to their tawny coats.

'I don't see any antlers,' Jennifer said as they drew nearer. 'Are those all females?'

'No, ma'am,' Clay said with a chuckle. 'The males shed their antlers in the winter and grow a new set every year that don't mature until autumn. They're just getting started now. See that big fellow looking our way? He's got the beginnings, if you look closely.'

Jennifer squinted, but could see nothing. 'I'm afraid I don't see that well,' she said. 'I can see that he's awfully big, though.'

'He'll probably have a rack seven feet across later on,' Clay said. 'Real trophy size.'

'Do you hunt them?' Jennifer asked, thinking of the moose head on the fireplace chimney in Clay's house.

'No, but there's a season on them. Have to keep the population under control or they'd eat themselves right out of their habitat. Which reminds me, I could use some lunch. Shall we head for the Johnsons' again?' Without waiting for an answer, he turned Ace and took off at a canter.

Midnight rocked along, her head held high, seemingly as tireless as a young horse. She loves this too, Jennifer thought. Everything seemed to thrive in the wide open spaces.

The Johnsons welcomed Jennifer and Clay into their home, Mrs Johnson commenting that it was nice to have company while the children were at school and they could carry on a real conversation for a change. After lunch they went to the calving shed, where a young heifer in the first stages of labour was being watched closely.

'It won't be long now,' Clay said after looking her over. He grinned at Jennifer. 'You'll get your wish within an hour.'

Clay was right. Jennifer watched, entranced, as two tiny forefeet and a pink nose emerged, followed rapidly by the rest of the calf. The new mother seemed a little surprised. She sniffed the calf carefully, and then began to lick it clean. In less than half an hour, the little bull was on his feet, looking for his mother's nipple.

'If only human children got on their feet that fast, it would save a lot of trouble,' Mrs Johnson commented drily. 'You could just feed them, put them down, and send them out to play.'

'That's from the woman who couldn't wait to have another one to rock in the rocking-chair,' Jacob Johnson teased.

The rest of the day went all too swiftly for Jennifer. She rode with Clay into the pasture where the other waiting heifers were kept, and met two cowhands who were on a constant vigil for signs of imminent delivery. Another heifer was taken in to calf, and delivered without any assistance.

'Good day, so far,' Jacob said. 'No problems. Let's hope our run of luck keeps up.'

The five Johnson children came home from school and plunged immediately into their chores.

'They're impressive workers,' Jennifer remarked. 'How do you do it?'

'There's no arguing about chores,' their mother replied. 'But they find plenty to argue about the rest of the time. We almost had a knock-out over which of the girls' rooms you'd stay in.'

By the time Jennifer went to bed on a camp-bed in

the room that two of the Johnson daughters shared, she felt as if she had known the family all of her life. What a wonderful place this is, she thought sleepily, just before she drifted off. Heaven couldn't be any nicer than a day at the Bar-C with Clay.

It was barely getting light outside when the sound of men's voices awakened Jennifer. She heard Jacob call out that he'd be right there, and then heard Clay's voice asking something about trouble. Apparently, she thought, the run of luck had ended. She crept quietly out of her camp-bed and dressed swiftly. She might as well find out what happened when things didn't go so well. A few minutes later she was on her way to the calving shed in the chilly morning air.

On a bed of clean straw, a black, white-faced heifer was lying, panting. Clay and Jacob were behind her, the device Jennifer had learned was a calf-puller attached to the forelegs of the calf. Its head and the front of its body had already emerged. Both men were resting, their heads down.

'What's wrong?' Jennifer asked, leaning on the half-wall of the stall.

'The calf's too big. It's hip-locked,' Clay replied grimly. 'I don't know. What do you think, Jacob? Shall we keep at it?'

Jacob pursed his mouth. 'We're going to lose one or the other, I'm afraid. I'm not sure the heifer's pelvis can take it. You decide.'

'Let's try and hope it gives enough,' Clay answered. 'If it doesn't, we'll have to put her down.' He shook her head, his expression bleak. 'OK, let's go. We haven't got much time.'

While Jennifer watched, Clay slowly turned the crank on the puller and Jacob tried his best to manoeuvre the calf into a more tractable position. Finally he, too, shook his head. 'Just give it all you've got,' he said. 'I'll get the hypo.' Clay grimaced and did so. Jennifer winced and closed her eyes at what followed, but she could not shut out the noise of the heifer thrashing and bellowing. When she reopened them, the calf was safely out, raising its head and looking around. The unfortunate mother was no longer in any pain. Clay was crouched beside her, one hand on her motionless side, his head resting on his other arm. A moment later he jumped to his feet and drove his fist into the side of the stall with such force that the wall shook. Then, his head down and his hands thrust deep into his pockets, he strode rapidly from the shed.

One of the cowhands, who was ministering to the new calf, looked up at Jennifer. 'He just ain't your average cattleman,' he said. 'You can't help but respect a man who cares so much.'

Jennifer nodded, tears in her eyes for both Clay and the hapless animal. Clayton Cooper was definitely not average. He was a man to both respect and to love. And she knew that she loved him with all of her heart.

CHAPTER SIX

FOR the first time since Jennifer had known him, Clay ate hardly any breakfast. He apologised for his lack of appetite, and then excused himself to go and see how the calf was doing.

'He'll be all right in a little while,' Mrs Johnson said, seeing Jennifer's worried expression. 'I've seen him that way a lot of times before. I'll fix you a lunch to take along. He'll probably get hungry before you get home.'

'I hope so,' Jennifer said. She longed to be able to go to Clay and hold him and comfort him, but something told her that he would not be receptive, at least for a while.

He was still glum when they rode away from the Johnsons'. 'I'll be all right,' he told Jennifer, trying to smile. 'Don't look so worried.'

'I'm not worried,' she replied. 'I just wish there were something I could do to make you feel better.'

Clay looked at her thoughtfully and then shook his head. 'Not right now,' he said. 'Let's cut over and follow the creek home.' With that, he put Ace into first a canter and then a gallop. After a time, he suddenly reined in his horse and looked back at Jennifer and Midnight, far behind. 'I'm sorry,' he said, when they finally caught up with him. 'I forgot you hadn't galloped before. I needed to get moving, to get some of the cobwebs out.'

'I'm all right,' Jennifer said, so relieved to see that Clay looked less depressed that she was not about to tell him how frightened she had been when Midnight had first broken into a gallop. 'It was kind of fun. But I think Midnight's tired. She's no spring chicken, you know.' The old horse was breathing hard.

'We'll take it easy now,' Clay said.

They rode on, Clay still silent, his eyes on the distance, seemingly oblivious to Jennifer's presence. She studied him, the way he effortlessly sat his horse, his back straight, his head with its strong, firm chin, erect and proud, the lord and master of this land. But his denim jacket was worn, his jeans faded, his boots scuffed from use. There was no doubt that he was a real cowboy, she thought, a real man. Would he break her heart in two? Never intentionally, she knew. But there was something in him, so wild and elemental and free. He wanted to be accepted on his own terms, or not at all. He had gone to considerable pains to make that point, as if it mattered a great deal to him that she appreciate him for what he was. But would he ever want a wife, or was Pam enough to satisfy any domestic urges he had? She sighed and looked away.

'There is better scenery to look at,' Clay said. 'I was wondering when you'd get tired of staring at me.'

Jennifer felt her cheeks grow warm. 'I'm sorry,' she said, giving him a sideways glance. 'I didn't mean to stare.'

'I'm not complaining,' Clay replied. He gestured towards a small cluster of willow trees just ahead. 'Those trees are on the creek. Let's stop there and have that picnic. I think I could eat something now.'

When they had dismounted, Clay unfastened the small wool blanket that he kept rolled behind his saddle and spread it on the grass next to the trees, which were just beginning to show their spring green. Then he produced the lunch from one of his saddle-bags, stretched out on the blanket, and patted the place beside him.

'Sit down here, Jenny, and tell me whether you think I'm a lunatic or not,' he said gruffly, staring up at the sky.

'A lunatic? Heavens, no. Why would I think that?' Jennifer asked, leaning on her elbow and looking down at him.

'Because I go through that same damn thing, over and over, no matter how many times it happens,' Clay replied. He looked at Jennifer. 'I thought maybe that was why you were staring at me. Wondering if I had a screw loose, or something. I think some of the men think I do.'

'Not the ones who were there,' Jennifer said. 'They respect you for feeling so strongly. One of them said so.' She smiled. 'I do too. I think you're very special.'

Clay smiled, that warm, intimate smile that set Jennifer's heart racing. 'Ah, Jenny,' he said softly, 'that's good to hear. When I was young, I used to worry that it wasn't manly to show my feelings, but as I got older I decided that it was far less manly to pretend to be something I wasn't just to fool other people.' He made a wry face. 'But maybe that's just because I'm stuck with being the way that I am.'

'I don't think you should feel stuck with it,' Jennifer said, reaching over to brush a wisp of hair back from Clay's forehead. 'I think you're lucky. I'm afraid many people don't feel things strongly enough, or they'd have more sympathy for unfortunate people and animals.'

'You may have a point there,' Clay said. He put his hand alongside Jennifer's cheek, and then slowly moved it into her silky hair and let it come to rest behind her neck. 'You're beautiful, Jenny,' he said, his eyes

searching hers intently. 'Sometimes when I look at you,
I can't quite believe you're real.' He began to pull her
slowly towards him. 'It makes me want to touch you, to
hold you close to me, so I can be sure.'

Jennifer offered no resistance as Clay pulled her into
his arms. This, she knew, was what she had been waiting
for ever since she had sat down beside him. She
stretched out next to him, her head on his shoulder,
absorbed in the intense blue of his eyes, now so close
to hers. She felt, she thought wonderingly, as if the only
thing real in her world were Clay. No splendour in the
world around her could possibly match the thrill of his
touch, the warmth of his smile. When his lips touched
hers, she closed her eyes and slipped her hand behind
his head, weaving her fingers into his thick, golden hair.
His tongue made a teasing circuit of her lips, and she
opened her mouth and met it with her own. With a deep
groan of pleasure, Clay possessed her mouth hungrily.
At the same time he turned on his side and moulded her
tightly against him.

Jennifer sighed with pleasure. In response, Clay
smiled and then trailed a stream of delicate kisses across
her cheek, beside her ear, beneath her chin. Even
through the thickness of their clothing, she could feel
the hard, massive strength of Clay's powerful thighs
pressed against her. He flung one leg across her and
turned her upon her back. She felt overpowered and at
the same time free, as if the wild singing in her heart
were a melody only Clay's touch could produce, a song
that sent her soaring like a bird. She grasped at his broad
back and held him tightly.

'My sweet little Jenny-wren,' he whispered, seeking
her lips again with his. He tugged her jacket open with
one hand and then slid his hand beneath it, first around

her soft sweater, a moment later beneath it. Jennifer felt her body tense momentarily, and then respond with a shiver of ecstasy at the touch of Clay's rough, warm hand. First he delicately caressed the bare skin of her ribcage, and then let his hand rest, cupped over her breast. He raised his head and smiled down at her, his eyes softly warm. Oh, Clay, I love you so, Jennifer thought, smiling into the delicious blue depths of his eyes. She felt a great surge of longing to have him closer, to feel his skin against hers. With one hand she tried to open his jacket, and when she failed he tore it open and quickly unbuttoned his shirt.

'Mmm, that feels so good,' he whispered, as he lay back over her, his lips nuzzling her soft neck. When Jennifer sighed and wriggled contentedly against him, he slid his hand beneath her and unfastened her bra. Very slowly he kissed his way downwards until his lips found the rosy peaks his hands had captured. Soft little sounds of pleasure escaped from Jennifer's throat as wave after wave of excitement built within her. Never had she felt such electricity. Beneath her closed eyelids, bright sheets of colour danced in rhythm to her soaring desire. Clay's lips went lower, until they reached the edge of her jeans. There, he paused for only a moment, while he unzipped her jeans and pulled them downwards.

'Oh, Jenny,' he groaned, as his hand explored and tantalised her. He pushed his own jeans down and then lowered himself upon her, moving against her with a fierce, eager motion, his burning eyes fixed on hers. 'I want you so very much,' he whispered, lowering his mouth to hers again.

Jennifer arched against him, dizzy with longing for the fulfilment she knew would come when Clay possessed her. She wanted to give herself to him, to belong to him, to bear his children . . .

Children! As if she had been doused with an avalanche of chilling snow, the fire inside Jennifer went out.

'Clay, stop!' she cried, trying to push him away. 'We can't! I can't!' At the sight of Clay's confused, hurt expression she burst into tears. 'I'm sorry,' she sobbed. 'I've never . . . it's not right . . . I might get pregnant . . . it's all my fault. I'm so sorry. Please don't hate me! Please!'

'Jenny, don't cry so,' Clay said, quickly sitting up and gathering her into his arms. 'I don't hate you. It's not your fault, it's mine.' He patted her back and stroked her hair comfortingly. 'I got carried away. I should have known better. It won't happen again, I promise. Don't be frightened of me, please. I'm not some animal who's going to punish you for being sensible. Jenny? Look at me. Stop crying now. Everything's all right.'

Jennifer looked up at him, tears dripping from her long black lashes. 'No, it isn't,' she sniffled, dashing the tears away with the back of her hand. 'I feel awful.'

'Well, if it comes to that, so do I,' Clay said with a grin. He glanced at the swift, icy waters of the creek. 'If it were summer, I'd jump in there, but right now I'm afraid it would freeze it right off.'

For a moment, Jennifer stared at him blankly. Then she caught his meaning. The twinkle in his eye sent her into a fit of giggles. 'That would be . . . terrible,' she gasped out, as Clay rolled her over and pinned her beneath him again.

'You bet it would,' he said, laughing. 'Eventually I think we're going to find it very useful.' He rolled them completely over again. 'Uh-oh, I think we just squashed the lunch,' he said. He reached behind him, pulled out the flattened bag and held it up. 'Shall we see if it's fit to eat?'

'Might as well,' Jennifer agreed. 'I think I'm hungry.'

They straightened their clothes, Clay so completely unembarrassed about getting himself together that Jennifer felt equally uninhibited. 'A disgusting little prude', Alan had called her, she remembered. He should see her now! They took out the sandwiches, which Clay decided were even better 'after a little hearty exercise'. He seemed in such good spirits that Jennifer wondered how they could have been better if they had actually consummated their relationship. Was he really that undisturbed by what had happened, or was he only trying his best to see that she felt no guilt or resentment? Whatever the reason, she felt so happy, basking in the warmth of his frequent smiles, that one thought came through, over and over, as clear as the blue sky above them. She loved Clay more and more with every passing minute. Whatever he had meant by his 'eventually', she hoped it meant that he cared for her too and would some day want to make her a permanent part of his life.

They started back towards the ranch, walking the horses and talking like old friends about the things they had done and the people they had known. Some inhibition between them seemed to have melted away, Jennifer thought, glad now that she had responded to Clay with such abandon. At least he could no longer doubt his ability to arouse her, if he had ever had any doubts.

It was late afternoon when they arrived at the ranch house.

'Well, well, back in time for dinner,' Nell commented wryly. 'Will wonders never cease?'

'Not in your lifetime,' Clay said, giving the round little woman a hug and a kiss which left her staring at him speechless.

Tanya, who was helping make salad for the dinner, gave Jennifer a knowing smile. 'I see you got the old Clay back,' she said. 'How did you do it?'

'I'll tell you later,' Jennifer said. It seemed a century ago that she had told Clay she wouldn't go with him unless he straightened up. 'Did you find what we were looking for today?'

'Not really,' Tanya replied, grimacing and shaking her head. 'There's still something missing.'

'What's missing?' Clay demanded, having hung up his coat and come back into the room.

'I'm not sure anything is, yet,' Jennifer replied evasively. 'It's probably just a matter of decoding Mr McDonald's system.' Which, she thought grimly, was beautifully set up to hide things, whether by design or sheer sloppiness she wasn't sure. 'I must say I'm not surprised you gave up trying to figure it out,' she added, to forestall the question she saw forming behind Clay's alertly sparkling eyes. 'If his books were as neatly organised as yours, there'd be no problem. But we'll get there.'

Clay frowned suspiciously and then shrugged. 'Let me know if I can help,' he said. 'I think I'll go and read the paper until dinner's ready.'

'Quick thinking,' Tanya murmured in Jennifer's ear, as she passed on her way to the table with the salad bowl.

Jennifer made a face and nodded. She knew Tanya was well aware that if there was an unexplainable shortage in the receipts from the cattle sales it was sure to start another huge row between the brothers.

After dinner, Jennifer went into the office with Tanya,

locking the door carefully behind her. 'I hope this place isn't bugged,' she said whimsically, looking around the room.

'So do I,' Tanya replied, 'and I'm not kidding.' She brought out the computer printout of the figures she had been working on during the day. 'First of all,' she said, 'I may as well tell you that the commercial contracts are in perfect order. The discrepancy is all in the cattle sold at auction. The funny thing is, there are no tickets from the auction house for the past year. They're usually sent along with the cheque, and have a record of the specific cattle sold, their price and weight. I don't know if Forrest would have kept those, but he might. All that I did find were the records on the bank deposit tickets and the bank statements. Those match up all right. Now . . .' Tanya took a deep breath '. . . multiplying the weight shipped by the average price they should have brought gives you approximately one million, two hundred thousand dollars. I read somewhere that a six or seven per cent weight loss, or shrink, might be expected, which should leave us with about one million, one hundred and twenty thousand dollars. From the records we have, that leaves at least another ten per cent missing.'

Jennifer studied Tanya's carefully documented figures. She remembered Clay's comment about Forrest paying cash for his big, new Mercedes, but carefully kept her face blank, rather than let Tanya have any idea of the chilling suspicion that had just entered her mind. That ten per cent would have easily paid for the car, with plenty left over for custom-made boots and suits.

'I guess,' she said slowly, 'that I'll have to talk to Forrest. I certainly hope he's got those auction tickets. Maybe the cattle all sold for ten per cent below the average price.'

Tanya shook her head. 'I doubt it. Bar-C calves usually go at the top of the range. We may be underestimating the amount.' She put her hand on Jennifer's arm. 'I know you're thinking that Forrest might have had something to do with making that money disappear, but I don't think he'd do anything that dishonest. I really don't.'

'I'm trying not to think anything ahead of time,' Jennifer said, looking into Tanya's troubled face. 'There are probably lots of possible explanations. Maybe the Bar-C scales are off.'

'Thanks for trying, Jennifer,' Tanya said with a sigh, 'but that's not likely. They have them calibrated frequently. Clay's a real nit-picker about that.'

'Well, try not to worry,' Jennifer said, putting her arm around Tanya's shoulders. 'I'll call Forrest in the morning and see if he can come over tomorrow afternoon. I'd just as soon he came when Clay's not here.'

'I'll skip that meeting, too, if you don't mind,' Tanya said with a grimace. 'Forrest wouldn't appreciate me prying into his financial dealings, especially if it looked as if I were pointing a finger at him.'

'I understand,' Jennifer said with a wry grimace. 'I shall face the music alone.' In the meantime, she would have to try to forget the whole thing, so that she didn't act nervous. She did not want Clay to get suspicious that there was anything amiss or he would surely start accusing Forrest. From what he had said about the Mercedes, he already had his doubts.

Forgetting was not too difficult, for when Jennifer and Tanya left the office Clay was playing the piano and Jennifer decided to go into his special room and see him in action. He was playing a Chopin waltz, rather slowly, Jennifer thought. Just as she entered the room, he hit a sour note and swore softly.

'My damned hand's all swollen from slugging that wall this morning,' he said, looking up at her and then holding his hand up for her to see. 'I am a genuine lunatic. There's no doubt about it.'

Jennifer examined his bruised hand and shook her head. 'I guess maybe I'll have to agree with you,' she said. 'Do you suppose you could learn to wear boxing-gloves when you're going to do that?'

'If I'm going to keep playing the piano, I'd better,' Clay replied.

'Do you always play classical music?' Jennifer asked, thinking of what Tanya had told her about Forrest's jazz ambitions.

Clay gave her a sideways glance. 'Tanya's told you about Forrest, hasn't she?'

'Mmm-hmm. I thought you told me he didn't play the piano.'

'I didn't say he couldn't play,' Clay said defensively. 'I meant that he didn't play the kind of music that won my mother's approval, and he resented the fact that I did.' He smiled wryly. 'I never told him, but I'd give anything to be able to play by ear the way that he does. You ought to hear him some time. He's really good.'

'But you never told him,' Jennifer said reprovingly.

'I guess I should, shouldn't I?' Clay said. He reached out and pulled Jennifer down beside him on the piano bench. 'You're going to reform me yet, Jenny, my girl,' he said, hugging her against him. 'How about a duet? Do you know 'Heart and Soul'?'

'That's the only thing that I do know,' Jennifer replied, laughing, 'and you might have to help me remember it. It's been years since I've played it.'

Clay started the bass rhythm, and pointed out the right keys to Jennifer. Soon they were going through the old song over and over. Pam heard them and came to join in on that and some other easy four-hand tunes.

'A wonderful day,' Jennifer said when Clay asked her if she had enjoyed it as they said goodnight in the hallway.

'One of the best,' Clay agreed. He framed Jennifer's face with his hands and kissed her lips very softly. 'Goodnight, little Jenny-wren,' he said. 'Sleep well.'

Jennifer went into her room, feeling so buoyantly happy that she wondered whether she would float near the ceiling instead of sleeping on her bed. If every day could be like today, she thought, she would ask little more of life. Except to be spending the night with Clay, too.

In the morning, Jennifer felt apprehensive about the call she was to make to Forrest, but apparently not enough to make Clay suspect anything unusual was afoot. After breakfast he gave her a hug and said he'd see her at dinner. He had some business in Bozeman that would keep him away most of the day.

When he had gone, Jennifer went into the office and placed her call to Forrest. He came on the phone, his voice silky.

'What can I do for you, Jennifer?' he asked. 'Or dare I hope you only wanted to hear my voice?'

'I'm afraid it's only business,' she replied, trying not to sound irritated. 'I need to talk to you about some of the ranch records that are relevant to your part of the business. Mr McDonald's records are so confusing and incomplete. Would you mind coming over this afternoon?'

'Not at all,' Forrest said smoothly. 'I'd be delighted. What time?'

'Two o'clock would be fine,' Jennifer replied. 'And please bring everything you have on the cattle sales for the past year.'

'I'll be there,' Forrest promised.

By the time that two o'clock drew near, Jennifer was on tenterhooks. The pitcher of iced water she carried to her desk to assuage her dry, raspy throat tinkled nervously in her hands. She had chosen that time because she wanted to be sure the cowhands who came in for lunch would be gone. Then she began to worry that Clay might get home earlier than expected. She had even gone to the trouble to look as plain and unattractive as possible, wearing a baggy sweatshirt and jeans, no make-up, and her glasses. Nevertheless, when Forrest arrived he glowed at her as if she were a film star.

'What an absolutely charming accountant,' he said. 'You look like a cute little college girl, about to do her homework.'

'Cut it out, Forrest,' Jennifer said coldly, closing the door behind him. 'We've got problems. Let me see what you've brought.'

'Problems?' Forrest said, frowning as he handed Jennifer two large folders.

'Yes, problems,' Jennifer replied, carrying the folders to the desk she was using. 'Please sit down,' she said, indicating a chair next to the desk. She opened the top folder and leafed through the pages. 'These are all records of the commercial sales. Don't you have anything on the auctions?' She looked at Forrest questioningly.

'I always turned all of that over to McDonald,' Forrest replied. 'It should be in the files here.'

'Including the auction tickets?' Jennifer asked.

'Yes. Why?'

'They aren't here,' Jennifer said, 'and we need them.'

'Would you mind telling me just what the problem, is?' Forrest asked, his voice suddenly much more like his father's and Clay's. Jennifer glanced at him. Strange, she thought. He even looked different, more like an earnest young man, concerned about his work. A regular chameleon.

'I'm still hoping there isn't one,' Jennifer said. She put the rest of Forrest's folder aside and brought out Tanya's printout. 'Let me explain what I've found,' she said. Very carefully, she went through the figures. Forrest, she thought, looked grim, but not especially guilty, as he grasped what she was telling him. 'So it seems,' she concluded, 'that at least a hundred tons of cow never got to the auction, or the money never got to the Bar-C account.'

Forrest frowned. 'Yes, it does, but I have no idea why.'

'None at all?' Jennifer asked sceptically.

'No. ' Forrest shook his head. 'I can't imagine why those figures are so far off.'

'That's interesting,' Jennifer said icily. 'And I can't imagine why you reported the same number of cattle sold as Clay did. Either a lot of them were as skinny as toothpicks, or you should have come up with a smaller number. How do you explain that?'

Forrest pursed his mouth into a grim line. 'I guess it never occurred to me that someone might be cheating,' he said. 'I just took Clay's total and wrote it down.'

'Oh, wonderful!' Jennifer snapped. 'Do you mean to tell me that you never checked the auction tickets against the numbers Clay reported, day by day?

Somehow I find that hard to believe. That should have been routine procedure for you.'

'Well, it's the truth, damn it!' Forrest said. He got to his feet and paced down the room, his head down. He looked so much like Clay had when the heifer had died, that Jennifer's heart momentarily softened. Then she remembered how badly he had used Tanya and it hardened again. Nevertheless, she tried to maintain a neutral expression as he returned and stood beside her once more.

'I have no explanation for what happened to those cattle, Jennifer,' he said earnestly. 'You've got to believe me. It would be crazy of me to try to cheat the Bar-C. I'm not clever enough to do that and get away with it, especially with a good accountant like you on the job. If my father were to find out I'd done such a thing, he'd write me out of his will so fast that it would make your head spin. After all of the years I've put in, trying to please him, that's the last thing I'd be willing to risk.' He bent and put his hands on Jennifer's shoulders, looking intently into her eyes, unaware that the door of the office had just begun to open. 'Please don't say anything to Clay just yet. Maybe we can figure out——'

Forrest did not get to finish his sentence. Clay suddenly appeared behind him. He grasped Forrest by the shoulders, spun him around, and delivered a smart right hook to his jaw. Forrest fell to the floor beside Jennifer's desk with a loud thump.

'Damn you, Forrey!' Clay swore. 'Do you have to try and get your hands on every woman in sight? I warned you to leave Jenny alone.'

'Stop it!' Jennifer cried, as Forrest struggled to his feet, his eyes narrowed, obviously ready to carry on the battle with Clay, who stood poised to deliver another blow. 'Forrest was here on business because I called him to come.'

Clay jerked his head around to look at Jennifer. 'Why? What did you need him for? Is he the clue to what's missing?'

'I don't know,' Jennifer replied, glaring at both men, 'but I'm sure not going to find out if you two keep this up.'

'So that's it,' Clay said, ignoring Jennifer. He gave a short, nasty laugh and leered menacingly at Forrest. 'I've known damned well that quite a lot's been missing, and who better than good old Forrey to pull some kind of trick with the books? That idiot McDonald was putty in your hands, wasn't he?'

'I didn't pull any funny business with the books,' Forrest growled, swinging wildly at Clay, who deflected the blow with his forearm. 'Some of the cattle never got to market, so maybe it was you that took them on a little side trip and pocketed the money.'

'Why, you dumb——' Clay finished his statement by shoving Forrest backwards.

Forrest staggered and then caught his balance. 'Watch out who you're calling dumb,' he growled. He flung himself bodily at Clay, knocking him to the floor and then trying to pin him down and pummel him.

'That does it!' Jennifer shouted. She picked up the pitcher of iced water and emptied it on to the brothers. 'Get up!' she snapped, as they both stared at her, startled and dripping. 'Now you two listen to me,' she went on loudly, as they got to their feet, looking sheepish. 'I doubt very much if either of you is responsible for those missing cattle. Shake hands, now, and apologise to each other. You're so much alike that it's ridiculous for you to fight.'

Clay frowned at Jennifer and then reluctantly held his hand out to Forrest, who took it with equal reluctance.

'That's a little better.' Jennifer glared at Clay. 'I can see why you hired me now. You wanted someone to do your dirty work for you. All you're really interested in is proving Forrest in the wrong. Well, I don't think he is, in spite of the way things look. At least, he's innocent until proven guilty. If you don't want to be fair, you can look for someone else to keep your books.' She looked over as Tanya appeared in the doorway.

'Oh, I didn't know ...' Tanya said, looking frightened at the sight of the two dishevelled men. 'What happened?'

'Just another episode in the life of the battling Cooper brothers,' Jennifer replied drily. She looked at Forrest, who was eyeing Tanya warily, and then at Tanya, who was now scowling at Forrest. 'This is getting to be entirely too much like home,' she said. 'I've had enough of family quarrels. I'm going to get some fresh air.' She walked swiftly out of the room and closed the door behind her. She felt tired and shaky, worried that she had again said the wrong thing. Clay had looked angry. Well, so what? He deserved to be yelled at. He had made her very angry!

Pam was just returning from school when Jennifer got to the back steps.

'How about going riding with me?' Jennifer suggested. Quite suddenly, the idea of riding swiftly with the wind in her face seemed very appealing.

'Sure thing!' Pam said enthusiastically. 'I'll change and meet you at the stables.'

There was something very soothing, Jennifer discovered, in abandoning oneself to the motion of a horse galloping across a field. It was fun, too, going

riding with the bubbly little girl, who was delighted to
have an audience for her excellent riding on her
well-trained little mare. By the time they returned to the
ranch house Jennifer was in a much better humour.
Perhaps, she thought, it would be a good idea to
apologise to Clay for losing her temper. After all, she
could hardly expect him to be better behaved than she
was. But Clay was not at home.

'He went riding off in one direction and then Forrest
drove off in the other,' Nell reported. 'He said he
wouldn't be back for dinner.'

'Is Tanya around?' Jennifer asked.

'She went for a walk,' Nell said. 'She looked pretty
unhappy.'

'Darn it all!' Jennifer exclaimed, unhappy herself.
She had probably just made things worse for that dear
little person. Oh, why hadn't she just walked out and let
those two ridiculous idiots to kill each other, if that was
what they were so intent on doing? She waited until
almost midnight, but Clay did not come home. At last
she went to bed, worried and depressed. Clay had to be
really angry with her this time. So angry that he didn't
want to talk to her at all.

CHAPTER SEVEN

'SEE you later,' was all that Clay said in the morning when he left. He had that look about him that Pam had described as 'about ready to explode'. Jennifer thought, wishing that he would and get it over with. Seeing him like that made a knot in her stomach that felt as big as a baseball. Tanya had not even come down to breakfast, which made Jennifer feel more miserable than ever.

'Some peacemaker I am,' she muttered to herself, as she wandered into the office, feeling sick and fuzzy-headed from a night of poor sleep. Troublemaker was more like it. She had better see if she could do something constructive for a change. Maybe if she compared Clay's records with the bank deposits she could get a clue about the mysterious shortage. If there was a systematic relationship between small amounts and particular loads it might tell her a lot.

She sat down at the computer and called up the file of Clay's data and compared it with the various amounts on Tanya's printout. 'Good heavens, that's odd,' she said, as she stared at the screen. It was as plain as day. All of the smallest amounts occurred when Barkley had been the driver. But he was such a shy, diffident man, a hard worker who, with several other cowboys, doubled as truck-driver. He apparently still lived as austerely as ever. How could he be connected to a shortage of over a hundred thousand dollars?

Jennifer chewed meditatively on her fingernails. Something just didn't add up. Mr McDonald was the one who had left suddenly. That might be expected of someone who had wanted to get away before the shortage was discovered. Especially if he knew where the money was, or had it himself. 'I wonder if he really did have a sick mother,' Jennifer muttered, as she got up from the computer. Maybe Nell knew something about the man.

'He was a real jolly type, up until the last couple of weeks,' Nell told her. 'I guess he was worried about his mother.'

'Worried about something,' Jennifer said, frowning. 'Where did he live? Did he have any special friends? I'd like to try and find him. He left a note that he'd send his address and telephone number, but he never did.'

'He and Barkley were as thick as thieves,' Nell said. 'They shared an apartment where the unmarried hands live. A real odd couple, I always thought.'

More than odd, Jennifer thought grimly. Either he and Barkley had co-operated in somehow marketing part of the cattle outside the auction, which sounded very difficult, or McDonald had set up his supposed friend. He could have opened another bank account somewhere where few questions were asked, deposited the full amount there, and sent a lesser amount to the Bar-C account. That sounded like a more plausible scheme for an accountant.

'I think I'll go and talk to Barkley,' Jennifer said. 'Do you have any idea where he might be today?'

'I heard Clarence say that one of the headgates at the branding camp needed fixing before round-up,' Nell replied. 'That's Barkley's department. It's way down in the pasture this side of the heifers, so unless you feel like a long ride you may as well wait until he comes back.'

Jennifer smiled. 'I never thought I'd say this, but I feel like taking a long ride. I didn't sleep very well last night. The fresh air might make me feel better.'

'Well, take it easy,' Nell said. 'You do look tired.'

'I'll be careful,' Jennifer said. She put on her jacket and Pam's cowboy hat and went to the stable, where Midnight's friendly whicker of greeting helped relieve her anxiety about taking such a long ride alone. 'We'll get along fine, won't we, old girl?' Jennifer said, rubbing the horse's soft nose. 'I can guarantee, we won't be going too fast.'

It was another beautiful spring day, the air so clear that it seemed to sparkle. The cool air relieved Jennifer's tired, feverish feeling, and she felt almost like a real cowgirl, sitting the saddle easily as Midnight cantered along. Thank goodness Clay had insisted she learn to ride. He had done so much for her, she thought, tears coming to her eyes. He had shown her a side of life she'd never seen before, made her laugh, held her close, and let her feel a depth of love she had never experienced before. If only she could get this business of the missing money and/or cattle straightened out and get back in his good graces, she vowed, she would never lose her temper with him again.

The ringing sound of hammering on metal came to Jennifer's ears even before she saw Barkley's old jeep parked near the complex of pens where the cattle would be brought on their way to summer pasture. When she drew nearer, she saw Barkley working with his portable welding outfit, a mask over his face to shield his eyes from the bright light. She reined Midnight in and dismounted a little distance away, waiting until Barkley raised the mask to make her presence known.

'Hello, Ms Tarkinton,' he said when he saw her,

bobbing his head and smiling shyly. 'Nice day for a ride.'

'It certainly is,' Jennifer agreed, thinking again that Barkley was the last person she would have suspected of being involved in some scheme to rob the Bar-C. 'I wanted to ask you something, so when Nell told me you were here I thought it was a perfect excuse to take Midnight out.'

'Ask me something? Oh, you mean about the inventory,' Barkley replied. 'I've got a complete list on the shop equipment for you, and I'm working on the spare parts now. I'll have that in a couple of days.'

'That sounds very good,' Jennifer said, almost reluctant to even ask the thin, earnest man about McDonald's whereabouts. 'Actually, though, I had something else to ask. Nell told me that you and Mr McDonald were good friends. I need to get in touch with him, and I wondered if you had his new address and telephone number. He forgot to send it to Clay.'

Barkleys' rather high forehead furrowed into a worried frown. 'Yeah, I've got those,' he replied, giving Jennifer a furtive look and then looking away again. 'Do you need 'em right away?'

'No, tonight would be fine,' Jennifer said, wondering whether Barkley did suddenly look very tense or her suspicions were leading her to imagine it. He had packed up a piece of welding rod, and was rolling it back and forth between his hands. In order to distract him from thinking that she had any suspicions about him or McDonald, she enquired about the massive headgate he was working on. 'How does that thing work?' she asked, gesturing towards it.

'The animal comes through the chute, sticks its head through, and before the rest of him can make it someone closes this around his neck,' Barkley replied, patting the large iron yoke. 'Has to work slick as a whistle, or the animal gets away.' He gave Jennifer a demonstration.

'That's fascinating,' Jennifer said. 'I never saw anything like that before. Well, I guess I'll ride back to the house. I'll see you later.

Barkley nodded, chewing on his lip as if he was trying to decide about something very difficult. 'Uh, Ms Tarkinton,' he said, as Jennifer started to walk away, 'is there something special you wanted to ask McDonald about?'

Jennifer paused. Was Barkley trying to find out if she knew anything, so that he could warn McDonald? She looked back and shook her head. 'No, just routine information,' she replied. 'One accountant to another.' She continued on towards Midnight, feeling as if Barkley's eyes were boring a hole in her back. I'm more nervous than he is, she thought to herself, as she swung up into the saddle and looked back. Barkley seemed to be going back to his work as if he wasn't worried at all. He didn't even see when she waved to him, the welding mask again covering his face.

She walked Midnight for a while, and then put her into her slow, comfortable canter. After a short time, she heard the sound of the jeep behind her. Apparently the efficient Barkley had already finished his repair work. She turned her head and looked back. Odd, she thought. The jeep was bouncing across the pasture towards her quite fast. Was Barkley trying to catch up with her to tell her something? She slowed Midnight to a walk again and watched, ready to stop if he signalled to her. Instead, he picked up speed, heading directly towards her. The jeep hit a bump, and one of the welding tanks flew up in the air and tumbled to the ground, but Barkley did not stop. Jennifer stared, her heart suddenly pounding. He was going to run right into her and Midnight!

She let out a yell and dug her heels into Midnight's sides. The old horse responded with a leap forwards, then burst into a gallop, flying across the pasture at breakneck speed. Crouched low over her neck, Jennifer was afraid to look back, lest she lose her tenuous balance. She knew Midnight could not keep up this pace for long. The jeep would surely catch up, and when it did . . . a sob escaped from her throat. Both she and Midnight would probably be killed. Poor, dear old Midnight, she thought, burying her face in Midnight's streaming mane.

'Turn, Jenny, turn!'

Clay's voice! Jennifer raised her head. Coming towards her on Ace, waving his hat frantically to his left, was Clay.

'Turn!' he yelled again.

Jennifer tugged on Midnight's rein with all of her might, but the frightened horse did not respond. 'Midnight, turn!' Jennifer screamed, pulling hard and leaning towards her right. At last, as Clay headed towards her, Midnight lurched to the right without slowing. Jennifer had the strange sensation that the world was suddenly turning sideways. Then she hit the ground and everything went black.

'Jenny! Oh, Jenny. Oh, lord.' Jennifer dimly heard Clay's voice above her. She heard a sob escape from his throat. 'I love you, Jenny,' he choked out hoarsely. 'I love you. Please be all right. Please. Oh, lord, why didn't I tell you before? I love you so.'

As if through a thick, chilly fog, Jennifer heard Clay's words and suddenly felt warm. Clay loved her! She forced her eyes to open, and through a swirling mist she saw Clay's tortured face. He mustn't cry, she thought. I'm not dead. And now I know that he loves me! She tried to smile, but her cheek felt numb.

'Jenny,' Clay said, bending close and peering into her eyes, 'don't move. I'll go for help. Do you understand what I'm saying?'

'Don't go,' Jennifer said weakly, lifting her hand towards his face. 'I'm all right. See?' She touched his cheek with her hand.

Clay caught her hand in his and kissed it. 'No, you're not,' he said firmly. He kissed her hand again and held it against his cheek. 'I love you, Jenny,' he said, 'and I couldn't bear it if anything happened to you. You may have a spinal injury and you must hold still until help comes. Will you do that for me?'

Tears of happiness trickled from the corners of Jennifer's eyes. 'I love you too, Clay,' she murmured.

Very gently, Clay touched his lips to Jennifer's. 'Please try to understand,' he said again, his forehead ridged with anxious lines. 'I must get help, and you must stay right here and lie very still.'

'Is Midnight all right?' Jennifer asked.

'Yes,' Clay said with a sigh, 'she's fine. She's grazing just over there.' He pointed to his left. 'Now, Jenny, listen carefully.' Again he repeated his urgent message that Jennifer lie still while he went for help.

Jennifer suddenly remembered why she was lying on the ground and panic seized her anew. 'Where's Barkley?' she cried. 'He'll come after us!'

'He's long gone,' Clay said. He started to get up.

'But I don't want to be alone!' Jennifer said, clutching at him. 'Barkley might come back.'

'No, he won't. He knows that I saw him,' Clay said

comfortingly. 'I'm going now, but I won't be long. Midnight will keep you company. Just lie very still. All right?'

'All right,' Jennifer whispered, tears still trickling from her eyes. She felt so strange, hot and cold at the same time, and her head ached terribly.

She heard Clay hit the saddle as if he had leaped on to Ace, and then Ace's hoofs thundered against the turf as he left at high speed. She stared at the sky above her, watching a few small white clouds change shape as they drifted along. With one hand she felt her ribs and chest, which hurt a little, but did not send any sharp pains through her. Her toes wiggled all right, and somehow she knew that was a good sign, even though it was very hard to remember just why. Mostly, she thought, she just felt terribly tired. Her throat, when she tried to swallow, hurt so much that she decided not to do that any more. Her eyes hurt too. Maybe if she closed them she could just go to sleep until Clay got back.

No, that doesn't help, she thought a moment later, quickly opening her eyes again. As soon as she closed them, she saw the jeep coming after her. She could even hear it, rattling and thumping across the rough pasture. But why could she still hear it? Her heart started to race. It wasn't her imagination! Barkley was coming back! She couldn't just lie here and let him run over her! He was getting closer and closer.

'I've got to run, if I can,' Jennifer panted, over the sound of her pounding heart. She pushed herself upwards, scrambled shakily to her feet and stumbled forwards, away from the sound of the oncoming jeep. 'I'm all right,' she said over and over. 'Gotta run. Can't stop.' She was getting away. She couldn't hear the jeep any more.

'Jennifer, for heaven's sake, what are you doing?' Clay shouted frantically from somewhere behind her.

Jennifer stopped and turned back. The door of Clarence's battered pick-up truck was standing open. Clarence was getting out of the driver's side. Clay was running towards her, his arms outstretched. 'Oh, thank goodness, it's you.' Jennifer took a step towards and collapsed into Clay's arms. 'I heard the truck,' she gasped, looking into Clay's distraught face. 'I thought it was the jeep again.'

'You poor little darling,' Clay said. He lifted her gently into his arms and started towards the truck. 'I met Clarence on the road and came back with him. He's radioed for the medical helicopter to come for you.'

'But I'm all right,' Jennifer said, clinging to Clay's neck. 'I don't need it.'

'You're going to go and get completely checked over,' Clay said firmly. 'We're not taking any chances with my love.' He nestled his cheek against hers and then drew his head back, frowning. 'You're on fire with fever,' he said. 'No wonder you're so pale and your eyes look so hollow. What were you doing out riding when you've got such a temperature?'

Tears came to Jennifer's eyes. 'Don't scold me,' she croaked pitifully. 'I've been feeling sick since yesterday, but I thought it was just because you were mad with me.'

'Oh, precious, I wasn't mad with you, I was angry with myself,' Clay said, his face anguished again. 'I knew I'd made a perfect ass of myself again in your eyes, and I was afraid you'd lost any respect you had for me.'

'You could have told me that,' Jennifer complained. 'I can't read your mind.'

'I guess I'll have to get over that habit of clamming up, won't I?' Clay said, smiling and dropping another kiss on Jennifer's pale cheek.

'Never let the sun go down on a quarrel,' said Clarence, who had been listening to the last of their conversation. 'That's the secret of getting along for a long time.' He gave Clay a meaningful look, and Clay grinned.

'I think you may have a good idea there,' he said. He cocked his head and looked upwards. 'The chopper's coming.'

'But I don't want to go to the hospital,' Jennifer said crossly. 'I've just got the flu.'

'Now, don't you fuss,' Clarence said, adding his voice to Clay's. 'You had a bad fall. If it's just the flu, you can come home and Nell'll play nursemaid.'

'And I'll ride along with you,' Clay promised. 'If you're all right, Clarence can bring the old Cadillac and we'll take you home in style.'

Jennifer was loaded into the helicopter as carefully as if every bone in her body were broken. But at the hospital X-rays revealed that, except for some bruises, all was well. Most of her aches and pains were from her high fever, due to a severely inflamed throat.

'Tonsillitis,' said the doctor, shaking his head. 'The worst I've seen in quite a while. You should have those tonsils out when you've recovered.'

'I'll see that she does,' Clay said, when Jennifer made no comment.

'That's what you think,' Jennifer muttered. After all of the poking and prodding and shots of antibiotics, she was not about to return to the hospital willingly. She felt too miserable to appreciate the gentle care with which Clay and Clarence bundled her into the back seat of the huge old limousine, wrapped in a big, soft blanket and nestled on several pillows. She dozed on the way back to the ranch, and was scarcely aware of being carried up the stairs and put to bed by Nell, who firmly ordered the men out of the room. Only one impression remained with her as she drifted into a deep sleep. It was the touch of Clay's lips against her cheeks and the sound of his deep voice.

'Sleep well, little Jenny-wren, and dream of me,' he whispered in her ear. 'Remember that I love you.'

CHAPTER EIGHT

'I DON'T even know what day it is, and I'm not sure that I care,' Jennifer said, when two days later she at last felt like sitting up and taking a little nourishment. She smiled at Clay, who was sitting on the edge of her bed, trying to feed her a bowl of soup. Having him close to her, knowing that he loved her, made her feel so warm and good that even the spectre of Barkley's pursuit seemed dim and far away.

'It's the first of that magic month of May,' Clay said, his eyes glowing with that special fire that made Jennifer's toes curl beneath her blankets. 'As soon as you're well, we'll take that ride up into the mountains that I promised you a long time ago. The wild flowers will be ready for you by then.'

'Mmm, that sounds lovely,' Jennifer said. She opened her mouth obediently as Clay offered her another spoonful of soup. After she had swallowed it she shook her head at him. 'You really don't need to feed me,' she said. 'I'm going to be terribly spoiled by all this fussing. Besides, you're neglecting your work.'

'*You* are my number one job,' Clay said, tapping her lightly on the forehead for emphasis. 'Besides, it helps alleviate my guilt for having let you go after Barkley alone. I should have been working with you instead of going off and letting you figure out by yourself the same things that I had. When I came home and Nell told me where you'd gone, I knew that was what you'd done.'

'What a strange man,' Jennifer said, frowning

thoughtfully. 'I'd never have believed he would be involved in something like that. Do you think the police will catch him?'

'Eventually,' Clay replied. 'They found the jeep, abandoned by the highway. Clarence thinks Barkley's still somewhere on the ranch. He knows it like the back of his hand. So while the police are scouring the rest of the county, we've got several of the cowhands looking for him here.'

Jennifer shuddered. 'I hope they find him. I certainly don't want to meet him unexpectedly again.'

'You don't need to worry,' Clay said, squeezing her hand comfortingly. 'Anywhere you go, from now on, I'll be with you.'

'That sounds wonderful,' Jennifer said, holding on to Clay's strong, rough hand. She sighed deeply. 'I certainly never expected to be right in the middle of a real chase scene. I'm not up to that kind of stunt riding.'

Clay chuckled. 'You were doing great. I think the only problem was that your saddle slipped. I'll have to give you another lesson on tightening the girth.'

'Maybe you'll just have to do it for me,' Jennifer said. She smiled at him sleepily. 'I think that's all I can eat. I feel like taking another nap now. I must be getting lazier instead of better.'

'That's because you can't be any better than you are,' Clay said, bending over to give her a kiss. 'Go to sleep, pretty one. I'll see you later.'

It was dark when Jennifer awoke again, feeling much more alert. She had just turned on her bedside lamp when Clay poked his head in the door.

'There's my girl,' he said. 'Do you feel up to having some more company? Pam wants to see you.'

'Of course,' Jennifer replied.

'I made you a get-well card,' Pam said, bursting into the room with her usual energy. 'That's supposed to be a picture of you riding on Midnight.'

'It's very good,' Jennifer said, smiling at the carefully drawn little picture. Inside, Pam had written, 'Get Well Quick, Jenny, We Miss You Downstairs.' 'Thank you,' she said. 'I miss being downstairs.'

As if to add to Pam's message, Nell and Clarence both came to visit, and Cookie brought up a special fruit plate which he had prepared so artistically that Jennifer told him she should frame it instead of eating it. Then Tanya came in with a bouquet of early tulips. When the telephone rang, Clay answered it and announced that his father wanted to talk to Jenny.

'I don't think I've ever been so popular,' Jennifer said, as she took the receiver. 'Hello, Matt. How are you?'

'The question is how are you?' the old man said in his hearty voice. 'My goodness, young lady, you gave poor Clayton a terrible scare. Guess he didn't know he hired a Wild West accountant.' Matt laughed heartily at his own joke.

'Wild West accountant?' Jennifer repeated, laughing with him. 'I think I'll put that on my business cards. Jennifer Tarkinton, Wild West Accountant.' She talked for several minutes to Matt Cooper, promising to call him the next day and inform him of her progress. 'What a dear,' she said, when she had hung up. 'Let's go and visit him as soon as I'm up and around. He says I've been neglecting him.'

'We'll do that,' Clay promised. 'Now eat your supper so you can get back to sleep and get well in a hurry. It's plain to see we've got to get you out of here. The Johnsons called earlier to ask how you were and there are six cowhands downstairs that are off their food because you're not at dinner. Pretty soon the ranch won't function without you.'

Jennifer smiled, remembering how she had at first felt a little strange at being given this room and made so much a part of this wonderful extended family. Now she wouldn't trade it for anything in the world.

In only two more days, Jennifer was back at the dinner table. Clay insisted on carrying her down the stairs because, he said, it made him feel very macho.

'It makes me feel like an invalid,' Jennifer complained, although she did not really mind. She was going to miss having Clay constantly at her bedside, fussing over her, playing card games with her, reading to her, and, most of all, making her laugh with his quick wit and sometimes silly jokes.

The following morning they visited Matt, who once again informed Clay that he had better marry Jenny.

'She's one in a million,' he said.

'Just be patient,' Clay said, his eyes brimming with both love and mischief as he looked at Jennifer. 'I'm working on it.'

'I'm too old to be patient much longer,' Matt grumbled. He looked thoughtfully at Jennifer. 'What's holding it up, girl? I thought you liberated ladies could propose to a fellow if he was too slow on the uptake.'

Jennifer blushed and then laughed. 'I'll think about that,' she said, giving Clay a sideways glance. Maybe, she thought, Matt had a very good idea. However, she'd wait a while longer. Clay looked as if he was planning something along those lines, and she would not want to spoil it for him. Perhaps it was connected with that trip to the mountains that he mentioned almost every day.

He mentioned it again the next day, grumbling

because a downpour had brought all outdoor activities to a halt.

'Well, we can do something else today, then,' Jennifer told him. 'I've been waiting for a chance to show you how Tanya and I have reorganised the Bar-C records so that you can understand them. I also need to explain to you what you've got to do to keep them up to date.'

'Hardly a substitute for a picnic in the meadow, but I suppose it will have to do,' Clay said resignedly. He sat down next to Jennifer at the computer. 'I haven't the slightest idea how to use this thing,' he said.

'All taken care of,' Jennifer replied, showing him a printed page. 'This tells you exactly what keys to hit in what order to get each of the files. Even a child could do it.'

'Mmm,' Clay said non-committally.

'Now then,' Jennifer went on, ignoring her reluctant pupil, 'I've made separate files for different kinds of expenses and income, and there is also one file which puts everything together from the data in those files, so that at any time you can see exactly where the ranch stands financially. There is also another set of files that make historical comparisons, and, if you want to work with me on it, we could try making projections. Now I'll show you what I mean.'

Jennifer then went slowly through the different files, trying to find out if Clay understood them. He made few comments, but at the end he let out a huge breath and shook his head.

'I think I'm going to know more than I ever wanted to know,' he said, with a rueful smile. 'That's terrific, Jenny.'

'Thank you. But here's the bad news. You have to see to it that we get the information on expenditures much more regularly than in the past. I found out that one of the cow camps only turned things in once a year. And you, yourself, do a lot of ordering of supplies without reporting it. Some of the bills are a complete mystery to me. It took me days to find out that floor chains had something to do with a hay baler. Try to jot everything down and give it to me once a month.'

Clay frowned. 'I'll try, but I don't guarantee anything. I don't like keeping records.'

'But you do a beautiful job on the cattle,' Jennifer said cajolingly. 'You can do it.'

'I can do anything if I want to badly enough,' Clay replied gruffly. 'I managed to keep a running balance in my head that told me something wasn't right, didn't I?'

'Yes, but it would have been a lot better if you'd been able to check McDonald's figures. If he'd known you were keeping a close eye on him, I don't think he'd have tried what he did.'

'If he did do it,' Clay said with a grimace. 'It was Forrey's job to keep track of the numbers that turned out to be wrong. I'm still not convinced that he didn't know what was going on.'

'Oh, Clay,' Jennifer said with a sigh, 'give Forrest a break. I can see from the records that you've put most of your share of the profits back into the ranch and he hasn't, but try to see his point of view. He wants to be doing something else. Imagine how you'd feel if your father had made you be an accountant instead of a cowboy.'

'I wouldn't have done it, inheritance or no inheritance,' Clay said stubbornly, 'and Forrey doesn't have to either.'

'I don't think you can say for certain what you'd have done,' Jennifer said, disappointed in Clay's response. 'It seems to me that you and your father both have a big blind spot where Forrest is concerned. You're both wonderful people in every other respect. Why don't you drop your vendetta against Forrest and go and ask Matt to let him do what he wants? Would it hurt you so much to do that?'

Clay got up and stood looking out of the window, his back to Jennifer. At last he turned around, shaking his head. 'My father wanted Forrest and me to share in the ranch only if we both worked here. It's not something I'd do to any child of mine, but I have to respect his decision. I can't ask him to change at this late date.' He came to Jennifer and took her hands in his. 'Don't look so sad, sweetheart,' he said, pulling her gently to her feet and into his arms. He smiled and rubbed one finger lightly under her chin. 'I know it doesn't make a lot of sense to you. I'm not sure it does to me. But I'm afraid it's not something you can change. I love you more than ever for trying, though.' He bent his head and peered into Jennifer's downcast eyes. 'Are you mad with me?' he asked.

'A little,' Jennifer replied. She laughed as Clay made an exaggerated pout. 'Clayton Cooper, you make the most ridiculous faces,' she said.

'I love to hear you laugh,' he said, rubbing his cheek against hers. 'And I love to see you smile.' He drew his head back and smiled, his eyes so warm that Jennifer caught her breath at the little thrill of delight she felt. 'And,' he added, slowly lowering his mouth to hers, 'I love to kiss your lips.'

With that, he possessed her mouth with such deep, fiery passion that Jennifer clung to him dizzily. She melted against him, feeling her own fires flaring, igniting a deep longing for more. Matt had a really good idea, she thought, as Clay's exploring hands made her sigh aloud with pleasure. If they didn't take that ride into the mountains soon, she was going to become very, very bold and liberated.

She was awake early the next morning, quickly possessed again by the thought of actually proposing to Clay if the weather prevented their trip. She went to the window. The sun was treating them to another spectacular sunrise, colouring the still snowy mountain peaks with a rainbow of soft hues. The sky was clear. Would today be the day? Jennifer was caught in a drowsy dream when a knock on her door startled her.

'Come in,' she called.

'It looks like a beautiful day,' Clay said, opening the door. 'Let's get an early start up the mountain. The morning mists are beautiful.'

'I'll get dressed right away,' Jennifer said, her pulse quickening. She could see by the suppressed excitement in Clay's smile that something was afoot, and she was almost sure that she was right about what it was. Matt was going to get his wish today!

When Jennifer arrived in the kitchen, Nell was busily packing Clay's saddle-bags with insulated containers of food.

'This is some lunch His Highness ordered,' she said drily. 'Don't eat too much breakfast.'

'Jenny never does,' Clay said teasingly. 'It's the bird in her.'

'Must be some hog in you, then,' Nell said, as Cookie delivered Clay's usual hearty breakfast. 'You two keep a sharp eye out. There's supposed to be a fifty per cent chance of more thunderstorms this afternoon.'

'Don't you worry, I'll take care of Jenny,' Clay replied. 'I know she's the one you're worried about.' He pushed away his plate, half emptied. 'I'm not very hungry this morning myself,' he said to Jenny. 'Let's get moving.'

Something was definitely afoot if Clay didn't eat, Jenny thought, her own nervous excitement increasing. 'I'm ready,' she said, putting on her new cowboy hat, which Clay had brought her for a get-well present. 'How does it look?'

'Terrific,' he replied. 'The Wild West accountant looks ready to ride.'

They saddled the horses and then headed off in the opposite direction from the Johnsons'. First they cantered side by side across another pasture, ghostly mists beginning to rise from the damp grass as the sun rose above the mountain peaks. Then they slowed to a walk, single file, as the trail started up the mountainside, weaving between the pines.

'Mmm, it smells good in here,' Jennifer said, inhaling the damp, piney air.

'I don't think there's any perfume smells as good,' Clay said, smiling back at her. 'I've always thought that the whole world should smell like this, so clean and fresh.'

'It definitely beats diesel fumes,' Jennifer said, taking another deep breath. How far away and unreal the city seemed on this beautiful day. If she had stayed in Chicago . . . no, she didn't even want to think about that. This day was hers and Clay's, and no one else's.

The trail wound higher and higher. The trees became smaller and more sparse.

Clay looked back. 'We only have a little further to go now, and it gets steeper. Just relax. Midnight's used to this trail.'

'Are there cliffs?' Jennifer asked apprehensively.

'I'm not good at heights.'

'Nothing to worry about,' Clay reassured her. 'Besides, heights don't bother Middle.'

He urged Ace forward. 'A little further' began to seem to Jennifer like a very long distance. Maybe, she thought, because the thought of threading along a mountainside like the donkeys she had once seen at the Grand Canyon made her very nervous. Her worst fears were realised when they came out momentarily on a rocky overlook. Up ahead, she could see the trail winding around the side of the mountain, appearing too narrow for even one horse to walk.

I'm not sure I can handle that even if Clay is going to propose to me after we get wherever we're going, Jennifer thought, biting her perspiring lip. She tried to smile when he looked back at her, but her lips were trembling, so it was not a very good effort.

'Don't look so frightened,' Clay said, giving her an encouraging wink. 'It's less than a quarter of a mile, and then we'll be at our destination.'

'I might not live to see it,' Jennifer said, making a face at him. With every step the horses took, they were drawing nearer to that tiny, rock-strewn ledge.

'Don't look down,' Clay suggested. 'Just look at my back. Or Ace's backside, if you prefer.'

'I'll try,' Jennifer replied, but as Midnight took her first steps on to the narrow trail Jennifer's eyes seemed compelled to look to her left, and down, down, down. A wave of sickening dizziness overtook her. It was miles to the bottom of the canyon. If Midnight slipped, if she were to fall off . . . 'I can't do it,' she said, pulling Midnight to a halt.

'Sure you can,' Clay said, stopping just ahead of her. 'I've done it hundreds of times, and so has Midnight.

She's a very sure-footed horse.'

'Maybe I could get off and walk,' Jennifer said. She could picture herself sidling along, clinging to the mountain with her back to the yawning crevasse. 'I think I'd feel safer.'

'You wouldn't be,' Clay said, now frowning at her. 'Middie's got four feet to anchor her, you've only got two.'

'She's got twice as many chances to slip,' Jennifer said sulkily. 'Don't frown at me. I can't help it if I'm an acrophobic.'

'You were a horse-o-phobic, too, remember?' Clay said, now grinning at her teasingly. 'You got over that. Come on, now, I guarantee it's worth it. Ask Midnight, if you don't believe me. Ask her if she wants to go.'

Jennifer grimaced and glanced briefly again at the bottomless pit to her left. 'Do you really want to walk along that tightrope, Midnight?' she asked, and smiled grudgingly as the horse bobbed her head up and down. 'How does she know to do that?'

'Mysterious powers,' Clay replied with a chuckle. 'Are you ready?'

'I—I guess so,' Jennifer said, trying to keep her teeth from chattering with fear. 'My life is in Midnight's hands. Or feet.'

They started forwards again. Jennifer kept her eyes glued to the centre of Clay's back. After a few minutes, she found herself watching his firm buttocks, rounded against the tight-fitting jeans he wore. Now that, she thought, actually smiling to herself, was worth watching. Maybe this trip was going to be more pleasant than she'd imagined. Midnight certainly didn't mind it, plodding along comfortably in Ace's wake.

'Here we are,' Clay announced, sooner than Jennifer

would have thought possible. 'Was it worth it?'

Jennifer stared, tears coming to her eyes at the beauty of the scene below. They were at a wide overlook above a long, narrow valley carpeted with flowers, and surrounded on all sides by steep mountainsides. A thin thread of a waterfall fell from the edge of the snow high above them, feeding a small stream which meandered across the valley floor and emptied into a tiny emerald-green lake. Through the mists, on the far side of the lake, a mule deer doe and her tiny fawn were drinking at the water's edge.

'This is the most beautiful place I've ever seen,' Jennifer said in hushed tones.

'I thought you'd say that,' Clay said with a smile. 'There's a wonderful echo in here. Want to hear it?'

'Oh, yes,' Jennifer said, delighted. 'I've never heard a real mountain echo.' Then she frowned. 'But it will frighten the deer away.'

'They'll be leaving in a minute anyway.' He raised his head. 'I love you, Jenny,' he called out, and seconds later the echo came back clearly, over and over.

The deer raised her head, then sauntered off, her fawn following, apparently not especially frightened. Jennifer then called, 'I love you, Clay,' laughing as the sound repeated itself. 'What fun,' she said. 'What a wonderful place.'

'It had to be a special place today,' Clay said, flashing a brilliant smile. 'And I think you know why.'

'I haven't the slightest idea,' Jennifer protested coyly. 'What do you mean?'

Clay only winked mischievously. 'Come on.' He clucked softly to Ace, and they moved forwards down a steep little path which led to the valley floor. Through the field of flowers they went, the horses up to their knees in lush, white-spiked bear grass, orange devil's paintbrush and blue gentian. In a cleared area near the stream, Clay stopped and dismounted. 'Come to me, my love,' he said, holding his arms up to help Jennifer down from Midnight's back.

Jennifer slipped off into his waiting arms, catching her breath at the deep warmth of love shining in Clay's eyes. Her arms went around him, holding him close, her face raised to his. She watched, enraptured, as his eyes scanned her face, glowing such a vibrant blue that they far outshone the sky above. He smiled slowly, then lowered his lips to hers, uttering a deep sound of happiness and pleasure at finding her waiting eagerly to share his passionate kiss. 'Ah, Jenny, I do love you so,' he whispered next to her ear. He drew back and held her at arm's length, smiling at her adoringly. 'I was going to wait until after we had lunch,' he said, 'but I can't stand the suspense any longer.'

While Jennifer's heart raced, Clay dropped to one knee in front of her and took both of her hands in his. 'Jenny, I adore you. I want to share the rest of my life with you. Will you marry me?' he asked simply.

Tears of joy filled Jennifer's eyes. 'Oh, yes, Clay,' she said. 'Of course I will.'

Clay let out a triumphant whoop and jumped to his feet. He crushed Jennifer to him and showered her face with kisses. 'You have just made me the happiest man on earth, Jenny,' he said. 'I'll try my best to be a good husband, as long as we live.'

'I hope that's a very long time,' Jennifer said, nestling against him, feeling so light and happy that she could scarcely believe she was still touching the ground.

'So do I,' Clay agreed. 'Forever wouldn't be long enough.'

He kissed Jennifer thoroughly again, finally saying raggedly that they had better have their lunch while he was still able to do such a mundane thing. He spread a bright blue blanket on the ground, and brought out the special feast of chicken and fresh rolls and a container of fruit, topped by a bottle of champagne which popped and fizzed with super effervescence in the high altitude.

'What a perfect day,' Jennifer said with a happy sigh. With their coats off, they were lolling in the warm sunshine, drinking champagne, kissing each other frequently and gazing dreamily into each other's eyes. 'Somehow, I never thought I'd be proposed to in a place like this when the right man came along. I always imagined it indoors, but I never could quite imagine the man I'd be with until I met you.' She looked at Clay thoughtfully. 'Maybe I shouldn't ask this, but somehow I can't believe that I'm the first woman in your life. You're not the shy, retiring type.'

Clay smiled wryly. 'I suppose you have wondered about that, since I'm not exactly a boy any more. Yes, there was another woman in my life, quite a while ago. At the time, I thought she was the right woman for me. I built the house, had so many plans. Fortunately, she decided someone else was the right man only a few days before we were to have been married.'

'Why fortunately?' Jennifer asked, frowning. 'It must have hurt you terribly at the time.' She remembered Clarence's early allusion to the unhappy, silent time at the Bar-C.

'It did, for a long time,' Clay admitted with a grimace. 'I was sure that no one else would ever fill her place in my heart. Overly romantic, I guess. But then Pam came into my life, and I learned what really caring for someone unselfishly meant. I began to feel very fortunate that I hadn't married earlier. And when you appeared, I knew I'd been very, very lucky.' He grinned boyishly. 'Think of all the luck it took to get you out here from Chicago.'

'It boggles the mind,' Jennifer agreed, laughing. 'What's the matter?' she asked, as Clay suddenly frowned and looked back over his shoulder.

'I thought I heard thunder,' he said. 'Maybe we'd better head back.'

'But I want to stay here forever,' Jennifer complained. 'This champagne has made me feel like dancing around the meadow.'

'OK, one dance before we go,' Clay said. He jumped to his feet and held out his hands to Jennifer. She grasped them, and then leaped up, squealing with delight as Clay led her in a wild polka around the meadow.

'I'm out of breath,' she gasped when he stopped. 'It must be the altitude.'

'And the champagne,' Clay said, nodding sagely. 'Come on, let's pack up the gear. I do hear thunder. We'll go back a different way, right out the end of the valley. That's the way the cattle come up here, and there's a cabin where we can take shelter if the rain catches up with us.'

'Do you mean,' Jennifer demanded, 'that we didn't have to go along that cliff?'

'That's what I mean,' Clay said. 'But wasn't it worth it to see the valley from above and to hear that echo?' He gave Jennifer a mischievous glance and began to repack the saddle-bags.

'I suppose so,' she said, folding the blanket and handing it to him. 'But what if I'd fallen down into the chasm? You'd have had no one to propose to.'

'I'd have dived right after you,' Clay said soberly. A

clap of thunder echoed around the valley. 'Let's go. It's coming in fast.'

Jennifer glanced up as she swung into Midnight's saddle. It looked as if a huge bowl of whipped cream were frothing up over the mountain peaks and beginning to spill down the sides. She had to put Midnight into a gallop to keep up with Clay as they thundered down the valley. At the end, a narrow passageway opened on to a fairly gentle slope along the edge of a canyon, the trail beaten hard and smooth by the hoofs of many cattle. The wind picked up, whistling along the canyon walls and making the tops of the pines thrash wildly. The sky grew dark and threatening above them, lightning flashes sending occasional moments of brilliance.

'The cabin's just ahead,' Clay shouted above Nature's roaring. 'We'd better stop or we'll get drenched.'

He had no sooner spoken than the skies opened up with a vengeance, sending sheets of rain flying almost horizontally through the canyon. Jennifer shivered, soaked to the skin almost immediately. It was with a great sigh of relief that she saw the little cabin, set back in the trees. Clay drew Ace up beside the hitching rack and dismounted, then took Midnight's reins and tied her as Jennifer slid from the saddle.

'Lucky I brought the key,' Clay said. He tucked an arm around Jennifer as he pulled a small key from his pocket and unlocked the padlock on the cabin door. 'In we go,' he said, and hurried her inside, slamming the door against the force of the wind. 'Phew! We almost made it.' He grinned at Jennifer. 'What a great adventure to add to our perfect day. Stranded together in a cosy little cabin.'

'I'd almost believe you planned it,' Jennifer said, looking around her, able to see only in the frequent flashes of lightning. The cabin was one large room, with a set of bunks, a pot-bellied stove with a ready pile of wood beside it, a table and chairs, and some minimal kitchen facilities.

'I would have if I could,' Clay replied with a grin. 'I'll get some lamps going and light the stove. Take off your clothes and we'll hang them up to dry. There's a clothes-line above the stove. This isn't an infrequent event up here.'

'Take off my clothes?' Jennifer cocked her head and frowned at Clay. 'And what, pray tell, shall I put on?' And what, she wondered, with a shiver of combined nervousness and excitement, did he plan to do when they had their clothes off? She was not sure she either should or could refuse him anything.

'Take one of those blankets over there on the bunks,' Clay said, as he lighted first one kerosene lantern and then another. He opened the stove, set the fire and then lit it. 'There. We'll soon be snug as a bug.' He grinned at Jennifer, who was struggling out of her sodden jeans. 'Need some help?'

'No, thanks,' she said, trying to clutch the blanket around her. 'Take care of yourself.'

'I intend to,' Clay replied with a chuckle. He quickly stripped, wrapped a bath towel around himself like a sarong, and then hung up his clothes to dry. 'I'll hang your things up,' he said, picking up Jennifer's soaked clothes. 'The line's pretty high.'

It seemed to bother him not at all, Jennifer thought, that his towel fell off twice while he was hanging up her clothes and he had to pick it up and tuck it back around him. She was sitting in a chair, still wearing her wet underclothes beneath the blanket, and feeling very strange at the sight of her husband-to-be, stark naked. She felt alternately like hiding her eyes and like staring unashamedly at his well-muscled, broad-shouldered physique. An almost unbearable longing to touch him made her clench her hands even more tightly around the blanket folds.

'Do you enjoy wet undies?' Clay asked, grabbing at his towel, which had started to descend again. 'Don't be shy,' he said, with a devilish twinkle at Jennifer's embarrassed look. 'I've seen girls before. And their underwear.'

'Oh, all right,' Jennifer said reluctantly, squirming out of her bra and panties beneath the blanket. 'But I might as well tell you that I haven't had any experience with naked men.'

'So I gathered,' Clay said, as he quickly clipped Jennifer's things to the clothes-line. He turned and came to stand in front of her. 'And I'll be very happy if I'm the only naked man you ever do have any experience with. Come here.' He beckoned with one finger.

'Wh-what for?' Jennifer asked, as she got to her feet, her heart beginning to skip erratically. The gleam in Clay's eyes was unmistakable.

Clay slowly put his arms around her. 'Well, it's going to be quite a while before the storm passes and our clothes are dry. We've got to do something to pass the time, and I sure don't feel like playing gin rummy.' He caught Jennifer's chin between his fingers and raised her face to his. 'Do you?'

'No,' she whispered, entranced by the soft, loving glow in Clay's eyes. She knew that they both wanted the same thing and she trembled, her lips parted, waiting for his kiss, already feeling the onslaught of excitement it would bring.

Very gently, Clay pulled her close, his arms still outside the blanket.

'I love you, Jenny,' he said, brushing the damp wisps of hair back from her cheek, his eyes scanning her face adoringly. He tucked his hand behind her neck and lowered his mouth to hers.

Like a flash of lightning more vivid than those in the heavens, Jennifer felt herself illuminated with a current of such strength that she let go of the blanket and clung dizzily to Clay's bare shoulders. His tongue swooped and soared within her mouth, seeking every nook of sweetness, drinking deeply with a passionate intensity that took Jennifer's breath away. He pushed the blanket from her shoulders and moulded her bare bottom towards him. She could feel the hot, hard insistence of his arousal. Its message turned on new waves of desire that flooded through her. She groaned, her fingers clutching harder at Clay's shoulders, her breasts feeling swollen as they pressed against his rough chest.

'Jenny,' he said raggedly against her ear, 'be mine now. There'll never be anyone else for me. But if you want to stop . . .'

'I don't,' she gasped, her heart filled with love for this man who could so easily overpower her, but who she knew would go no further if she but said the word. 'I belong to you, too,' she said, smiling mistily.

Clay looked down at her and said very softly, 'Thank you, my love.'

He lifted her into his arms and carried her to the bunk. 'Not the luxury I'd planned for our first lovemaking,' he said, as he nestled Jenny against him, his hands stroking her with tantalising lightness.

'Somehow it seems perfect,' Jenny replied, caressing

his cheek. 'I like being in a cowboy's cabin with a real cowboy.'

'I'd like being anywhere with you,' Clay said, his lips seeking hers again. He showered her face with kisses and then moved to tease his way downwards with more soft kisses and explorations of his hands that sent Jennifer into a dream world of beautiful sensations.

'Oh, Clay,' she murmured, as he stroked her thighs and then moved above her. 'I want you so much. I've never felt like this before. It's so much better than I ever dreamed.'

'The best is yet to come,' he said, gazing down at her with eyes filled with love as he very gently entered her and made her a part of him. Then, building rapidly in response to Jennifer's moans of pleasure, he led her along a trail which soared past the earthly mountain-tops into a new realm where a more beautiful sunrise than any she had seen burst forth and sent her into a world filled with unsurpassed beauty. When at last Clay lay still upon her, Jennifer stroked his hair, tears of happiness in her eyes.

'That was so wonderful,' she whispered, afraid that a louder sound would break some kind of magical spell. 'No wonder whole kingdoms have been thrown away for love.'

'Mmm-hmm,' Clay murmured drowsily. 'Shall we stay here until morning? No one will worry. They'll know where we are. And then we can go home and give everyone the good news.'

'That's a lovely idea,' Jennifer said, nuzzling her lips against his cheek. 'Let's do it.'

CHAPTER NINE

'I FEEL as if we've already had our wedding night,' Jennifer said in the morning as they started back towards the ranch. She felt light and airy, and yet somehow fulfilled, as though something within her had at last found its place in the world.

'That will be hard to top,' Clay agreed with a grin, 'but I'll think of something.'

They galloped across the last field before home in high good spirits, singing 'Oh, What a Beautiful Morning' as they went.

'Funny that Clarence is still here,' Clay remarked with a frown as they approached the back door of the house.

'I hope they're not worried about us,' Jennifer said. 'It is a little late.'

They hurried into the kitchen, both ready with smiles to tell their news. At the sight of Barkley sitting beside Clarence, his head down, they stopped. Jennifer's heart leaped into her throat at the memory his face brought back. She stood, immobile, while Clay advanced to the table.

'So you caught him,' Clay said to Clarence. 'Good work.'

'Not exactly,' Clarence replied drily. 'He showed up, trying to sneak back into his place and get some of his stuff. Didn't put up any fight at all when I found him. He says he's got something to tell you.'

'And I've got quite a few questions for him,' Clay

replied grimly. He pulled out a chair and sat down across from Barkley, who still avoided his eyes. Jennifer walked slowly across the room and stood a little distance behind Clay, waiting nervously. 'OK, Barkley, out with it,' Clay said. 'I assume what you're going to tell us has something to do with the shortage that both Jenny and I found on the days when you drove for us. I want to know exactly what happened, how you did it, and who was in it with you. I don't think you're smart enough to have made over a hundred thousand dollars disappear without a trace.'

Barkley folded his bony hands together in front of him and looked up furtively at Clay. 'I don't know where the cattle went,' he said. 'It was all Forrest's idea. He made the arrangements, and I never knew who the people were. I'd stop on a side-road, unload some cattle into a trailer that was waiting, and then go on to the sale barn. I never saw none of the money. I just got to keep my job if I didn't say nothin'.'

Jennifer could see Clay's back stiffen. 'It was Forrest's idea? He got the money?' he asked in a voice that sounded as cold as a glacier.

'Yep,' Barkley replied, looking down at his hands. 'He got it all.'

Clay pushed his chair back with such force that it toppled into Jennifer. 'That rotten son of a bitch,' he growled. He turned towards Jennifer, his eyes flashing. 'That does it. I'm going to nail that low-down cheating brother of mine to the wall right now!' He started past Jennifer, but she caught at his arm.

'Where are you going?' she cried. 'What are you going to do?' Visions of a real shoot-out sent shivers of terror through her.

'I'm going to throw him off the ranch,' Clay said,

flinging Jennifer's hand away. 'You stay here. You won't like watching what's going to happen.'

'I will not stay here!' Jennifer said, running along to keep up as Clay strode rapidly through the door and towards the garage. 'Someone's got to try and talk some sense into you.'

'Drop it, Jenny,' Clay said, his eyes dark and glittering with a cold hatred as he glanced at her. 'This isn't your fight.' He leaped into his pick-up truck and slammed the door.

'It is if I'm going to marry you,' she replied, wrenching open the door of the pick-up and getting in beside him. 'For heaven's sake, Clay, try to use a little common sense,' she shouted, as they roared down the drive. 'You have only Barkley's word for what happened. I still think it's McDonald who's behind the whole thing. He's the one who disappeared without a trace. Everyone knows Forrest. How could he arrange anything like that in complete secrecy?'

'I could manage it. He probably could too,' Clay said grimly. 'Besides, why would Barkley protect McDonald? That makes no sense at all. What does make sense is that Forrest used my figures on the number of cattle shipped to hide what he was doing.'

'I don't know why Barkley would protect McDonald, but I'd certainly like a chance to find out!' Jennifer snapped. 'And it is possible that Forrest was simply sloppy in his procedures because he didn't think anyone would cheat.'

'Oh, come on, Jenny,' Clay said in scathing tones. 'You know better than that.'

'No, I don't, and neither do you!' She took a deep breath. 'Please, Clay,' she said in softer tones, 'let's turn around and go home. You're in no condition to talk to

Forrest right now. At least take some time to calm down.'

'I am not going to get more calm,' Clay replied stubbornly. 'I will only get more angry by the minute!'

Tears of anguish filled Jennifer's eyes. Why, oh, why did this have to happen right now, just when she and Clay were so happy? Damn Barkley anyway. Why didn't he just stay away?

The truck careened to a stop before the old ranch house. 'Why don't you just stay in the truck?' Clay suggested, his expression softening for a moment. 'I'll deal with Forrest and be back in a few minutes.'

Jennifer wavered, a stream of conflicting thoughts pouring through her mind. Why not just avoid watching Clay deal such a blow to his brother? With Forrest gone, she could pretend it had never happened. But it was so unfair! Tanya was sure that Forrest could never be dishonest. Why, when he had cheated on her? Still, Forrest had seemed sincere enough when he'd denied to her that he knew anything about the missing thousands. Was he just a very good liar? She shook her head.

'No, Clay, I want to see how Forrest reacts,' she said. If he looked guilty, or admitted the scheme, then maybe she could forgive Clay for his temper.

She followed Clay into the house, which he entered without knocking on the door. 'Where's Forrey?' he demanded of the housekeeper, who came scurrying to see who was there.

'He's talking to your father,' Mrs Young replied, looking anxious at the sight of Clay's dark scowl. 'Don't you upset your father, now,' she warned.

'He's got to learn the truth sooner or later,' Clay said grimly.

'Clay, no!' Jennifer cried. 'Not in front of Matt!' She tried to grab his arm, but he shook her off impatiently and strode down the long hallway as if he were marching into battle. He flung open the door to Matt's room and walked over to Forrest, who was sitting in an easy chair near the bed. Jennifer stayed in the doorway, wringing her hands in agony.

'What's up, Clay?' Forrest asked, looking up, a curious frown between his brows.

'The game's up, Forrey,' Clay said, his voice hard and cold. 'Barkley told us how you did it. I doubt there's any chance of the Bar-C getting the money back, so I suggest you just pack your bags and get out of here. And stay out.' He glanced over at Matt. 'Of course, it would be nice if you had the good grace to apologise to our father before you go.'

'What in hell are you talking about, Clayton?' Matt demanded. 'What's all this about getting money back?'

'Tell him, Forrey,' Clay said, his lip curling in disgust. 'Tell him how you marketed some of the cattle that you had poor old Barkley steal from us.'

'I did no such thing!' Forrest said, jumping to his feet and glaring at Clay. 'I don't know where you ever got such a wild idea, but——'

'Directly from Barkley,' Clay interrupted. 'Jenny and I found a suspicious shortage on the loads he drove. That's apparently why he tried to run her down. To protect you, you worthless fool.' He leaned menacingly towards Forrest. 'How in heaven's name could you do such a thing to this ranch that our father and I have worked so damned hard to make succeed?'

'Damn it, Clay, I had nothing to do with Barkley!' Forrest cried, his face agonised as his eyes darted from Clay to his father and back. 'I barely know the man!

What in hell am I supposed to have done?'

Clay repeated Barkley's story. 'Pretty clever,' he concluded grimly, 'but not clever enough.'

'The man's lying,' Forrest said, shaking his head. 'That's an out and out lie. And you're a bastard for believing him.'

'Don't call names,' Clay snarled, grabbing Forrest by the shirt front.

'Stop it right now!' Jennifer shrieked. 'Look at your father!' Matt was sitting forward, clutching at his chest, pale and gasping for breath. 'Get the nurse!'

Clay let go of Forrest and ran from the room, reappearing moments later with the nurse in tow. She hurried to the old man's bedside and grasped his arm to take his pulse. Quickly she dropped his arm and took up a waiting hypodermic needle and inserted it into his arm. 'There, there, Matt,' she said, as the old man seemed to relax almost instantly. 'It'll be all right now. You shouldn't get so wrought up, dear.'

'Get those two out of here,' Matt growled. 'And keep 'em out. Jenny, come here.'

Jennifer walked very slowly to the old man's bedside, her heart aching as if it had broken in two. As she'd watched Clay and Forrest, a terrible chill had gone through her. Nothing that she could do or say would stop them from their endless battle. She was convinced that Forrest was innocent this time and that eventually Clay would admit that, too. But there would be something else for them to fight over after that, and after that, and after that. For all that she loved Clay, she could not stay and watch them, year after year.

'Feeling better now, Matt?' she asked softly, taking the old man's hand in hers.

'Not much,' he replied with a grimace. 'I don't know

what to do with 'em, Jenny. Do you think you can straighten them out?'

'I'm afraid not,' she replied, shaking her head. 'I've tried, but . . . I don't want to keep trying. I want to go somewhere where people don't fight.' She smiled ruefully. 'Even if that means I have to spend my life alone with only a cat for company.'

Matt looked at her thoughtfully. 'I don't blame you, Jenny,' he said, squeezing her hand. 'I don't blame you one bit. Does that mean you're leaving us?'

Tears sprang to Jennifer's eyes at his words. Yes, it did mean that, she thought. It meant the end of her beautiful dream. 'I'm afraid so,' she said hoarsely, tears spilling down her cheeks.

'Now don't you cry, young lady,' Matt said firmly. He pulled Jennifer towards him. 'Look me in the eye, and listen.' When Jennifer complied he nodded. 'That's better. I know you feel really bad right now, but it won't last forever, no matter what you think. Besides,' a twinkle came into his kindly old eyes, 'I have a feeling this might be a beginning for you, not an end.'

'That's a nice thought,' Jennifer said, sniffling back her tears. She bent and kissed Matt's cheek. 'I'm going to miss you,' she said. 'If you get better, give me a call. I'll be available.'

Matt chuckled. 'By golly, I might just do that,' he said. 'Now, I know Clayton's going to fuss at you something terrible when you tell him you're leaving, but don't let it stop you. You're on the right track. Some things aren't to be borne, and there's no reason why you should wear yourself out trying.'

Jennifer nodded. 'Thanks, Matt. I'll try to remember.'

'One other thing,' Matt said, a wicked gleam in his

eyes. 'Tell those boys that I don't want to see either of them again.'

'Now, Matt,' Jennifer scolded. 'That won't help, either.'

'I'm not so sure,' he replied. 'You tell 'em for me.'

'All right,' Jennifer said with a sigh. Then she turned and hurried from the room.

Clay and Forrest were waiting in the hallway.

'Is he all right?' Forrest asked anxiously.

'Can I see him now?' Clay asked.

'I'm afraid not,' Jennifer replied. 'He's all right, but he doesn't want to see either of you. Ever again. He told me to tell you that.'

Clay grimaced and glared at Forrest. 'Now see what you've done?' he said accusingly.

'I didn't start anything,' Forrest replied. He looked closely at Jennifer. 'You've been crying. What's wrong?'

Jennifer looked back and forth between the brothers. Should she wait and tell Clay alone of her decision to leave instead of marrying him, or should she drop the bombshell right now? No, she decided, even though it was tempting, that would be too cruel and too degrading in front of Forrest. 'It's something that I need to discuss with Clay,' she said. 'He'll tell you about it, I'm sure.' With that, she walked on down the hallway and out of the door to the truck.

When Clay got into the truck, Jennifer could tell from his bleak expression that he was still thinking about his quarrel with Forrest and was very little concerned with what had made her cry. That being the case, she might as well pack her bags and be ready to go when she told him of her decision. That would make it harder for him to stop her.

Clay was grimly silent all the way back to his house.

'I think I'll go for a ride,' he said, after he had parked the truck. 'Tell Nell not to wait dinner for me.' He turned and walked away.

Jennifer stared after him. He seemed oblivious to her existence. Should she tell him, or just leave a note behind? No, that was the cowardly way out. 'Wait a minute, Clay,' she called. 'There's something I have to tell you before you go.'

'What is it?' he asked impatiently, turning and waiting while Jennifer walked up to him.

Her hands clenched tightly, her heart pounding, Jennifer stood in front of the man she loved and looked up at him. 'I won't be here when you get back,' she said. 'I can't marry you, Clay. I'm going back to Chicago on the first plane I can get.'

'You're . . . you're what?' Clay asked, dumbfounded.

'I'm going back to Chicago. I can't marry you,' Jennifer repeated. 'I think you know why.'

'But, Jenny . . .' Clay grasped at her shoulders, his face anguished. 'Jenny, you can't do that! Please, don't give up on me. I love you. I can't live without you. I'll do anything you ask. Please.'

'I already asked, Clay,' Jennifer said, tears now running unchecked down her cheeks. 'It didn't do any good. Goodbye.' She wrenched herself free of his grasp and ran, sobbing, to the house.

CHAPTER TEN

AS THE plane lifted off from the runway, Jennifer closed her eyes, feeling sick and exhausted. 'Am I doing the right thing?' she asked herself over and over. Each time the answer was an agonised, 'I don't know!'

Clay had tried his best to persuade her to stay, declaring his love repeatedly, promising never to fight with Forrest again.

'I don't think you can promise that,' Jennifer told him. 'I'm not sure it's something you can control.'

Clay had become angry then. 'I think the fact that I fight with my brother is one hell of a reason to give up on a lifetime of happiness.'

'I agree,' Jennifer had said meekly. 'But I can't help the way it makes me feel. Maybe I'll see a psychiatrist about it.'

The only things that buoyed her spirits a little were Matt's advice to follow through on her decision, and Tanya's understanding. Tanya had driven the still weeping Jennifer to the airport. 'Hang in there, Jennifer,' she said comfortingly. 'I think you're doing the only thing you can do right now, and I don't blame you a single bit. Maybe your leaving will actually get those two idiots to look at what they're doing for a change. I still have hopes that some time they'll try to see how it all started and then I might have my sweet, funny Forrest back again. He's really such a gentle soul.'

'I've had that impression, too,' Jennifer said

thoughtfully. 'I guess I don't really know as much as you do about their history. When did they start fighting? Clay said Forrest started to change because he couldn't compete with Clay's success in some rodeos when they were in college.'

Tanya shook her head. 'That was only part of it. The main problem was, and still is, that Forrest knuckled under to Matt's demands. He's just not the fighter that Clay is, and I don't think Clay has ever understood how he could do that. He lost his respect for Forrest right then. I think that if Forrest had defied Matt and done what he wanted to, Clay would have gone to bat for him with his father and eventually convinced him that he was wrong. Clay's always been Matt's pet. But Forrest was afraid of the old man's wrath even more than he was worried about losing his inheritance.'

'I think he might have been surprised at Matt's response if he had defied him,' Jennifer said. When she had had time to think about it, the fact that he'd encouraged her to leave had struck her as odd, considering the way he had insisted that she marry Clay. Of course, he hadn't known how close she came to fulfilling his wish. 'I think Matt respects people who have the courage of their convictions.'

But, Jennifer thought sadly, as the plane soared high above the mountains, she wasn't sure that she had enough courage to see her through. Fortunately, her mother had sounded in a good humour when she'd called to announce that she was coming home. At least she wasn't walking into the middle of one of her family's all too familiar fights.

She was mildly surprised to find both of her parents waiting to greet her at O'Hare International, both full of concern over her tired appearance. She was even more surprised to enter the house where she had grown up in Oak Park and find that it had been completely redecorated. That, combined with her parents' happy chatter on the drive home, suddenly struck her as very unusual.

'What's going on here?' she asked, looking around at the bright new paint and pretty country-style furnishings. 'Did you win the lottery or something?'

'Not exactly,' her mother said, gazing lovingly up at her tall husband. 'Your father and I decided it was time for a new beginning. We've been going to a marriage counsellor, too, and it's like a honeymoon all over again.'

'It certainly is,' Jennifer's father said, giving his wife a warm hug. He looked at Jennifer and smiled ruefully. 'When you left the way you did, we took stock of our lives and decided that maybe we ought to try and make some improvements. It didn't feel very good to have our lovely daughter want to get as far away from us as she could.'

'No, it didn't,' her mother agreed fervently. 'I do hope . . . that is, will you stay with us for a while? At least until you find a new job?'

Jennifer stared at them, almost unable to believe what she had heard. A huge lump formed in her throat. She ran to them and threw her arms around both of them. 'Of course I will,' she choked out, burying her face in her father's shoulder. Then the dam burst, and she sobbed uncontrollably.

'Baby, come and tell us what's wrong,' her mother said, patting Jennifer's shaking shoulders. 'Come and sit between us on the sofa. There, there, it's all right. We'll help you, whatever it is, won't we, dear?'

'Of course we will.' Her father sat down on the other

side of Jennifer and put his arm around her. 'Just relax, sweetheart, and tell us when you can.'

Jennifer nodded, her sobs slowly subsiding. Haltingly, she began her story, realising that it was going to hurt these two dear people who were trying so hard to change to find out that their past quarrels were involved in their daughter's unhappy departure from Montana. She saw how deeply it hurt, when, at the conclusion, her mother burst into tears.

'Oh, Tom,' she said, reaching across Jennifer and clutching at her husband's hand, 'it's our fault! If only we'd had the sense to see what we were doing to Jennifer sooner!'

'There's no use to cry over spilled milk,' Tom Tarkinton said firmly. 'Let's try and look on the bright side. If Clayton Cooper cares as much for our Jennifer as we do, then maybe he and his brother will settle their differences.'

'I don't know if they have marriage counsellors for brothers,' Jennifer said with a sigh, 'but maybe there's some hope, after all.' Never in her wildest dreams had she imagined that her parents could reform after so many years.

'Oh, we still argue now and then,' her mother said the next morning, as she and Jennifer lingered over coffee in the bright new breakfast alcove that had been added to the old brick house. 'The counsellor says you can't expect to never disagree. But there are no more tantrums and shouting, dishes breaking, or doors slamming when someone leaves, threatening to never come back.'

'I'm so happy for you,' Jennifer said. 'It's almost enough to make me forget my troubles. But why didn't you write and tell me about everything?'

'I just started a long letter to you yesterday,' her

mother said. 'I didn't want to say anything, until we were sure we were really on the right track. I'll show it to you.'

Jennifer watched her still young-looking mother hurry from the room, a lightness to her step that was so touching that Jennifer felt tears come to her eyes.

'There's some shocking news in there,' her mother said, as she returned and handed the letter to Jennifer. 'It's about Alan Bailey.'

'Oh?' Jennifer turned her attention to the letter. 'Good heavens,' she said, looking at her mother. 'When did that happen?'

'Just after you left. He started dating the girl who brought charges against him right away, I guess. But would you ever have believed he'd turn that sadistic?' Mrs Tarkinton's eyes were wide with amazement.

'Yes, I would, Mother,' Jennifer said sadly. 'Remember my black eye?'

'No! He didn't!'

'Yes, he did. I should have told you then. I didn't leave only because of you and Daddy fighting. I wanted to get far away from Alan, too.'

'And I thought he was such a gentleman. You never know, do you?' Mrs Tarkinton shook her head. 'I'm sorry I pushed you to marry him. I should have trusted your judgement.' She looked at Jennifer appraisingly. 'I get the impression that Clay Cooper is still at the top of your list. Am I right?'

'Yes,' Jennifer said with a sigh. 'He's a very special man.' She went on to tell her mother about Clay and the ranch, leaving out nothing except the night she and Clay had spent in the cabin.

'What an exciting place!' Mrs Tarkinton said. 'I'm afraid Chicago is going to seem terribly dull after the

Bar-C Ranch. Do you plan to look for another job here, or just wait and see what happens out west?'

'I don't think there's any point in waiting,' Jennifer replied. 'Who knows if anything will change? But I do think I'll wait for a few weeks before I start job hunting. Clay paid me for the next month, even though I didn't want him to.'

'Good idea,' Mrs Tarkinton agreed. 'You need to rest and get back in the swing of things. We'll keep busy, too. Sitting around and brooding is the worst thing you could do.'

For the next several weeks, Jennifer obediently followed her mother on shopping expeditions, took trips to the Lake Michigan beaches with both parents, and generally felt like a child again, enjoying a new look at life. Still, she could not get over the gnawing ache that possessed her whenever she thought of Clay, an ache that grew ever stronger instead of weaker. Nor did she seem to be feeling more energetic.

'I don't know why I'm so tired all of the time,' she complained one morning, poking listlessly at the cereal before her. 'Nothing tastes very good, either. I guess I'm what the cowboys call "off my feed".'

'Maybe you should see a doctor,' her mother said, frowning. 'I've noticed that your eyes look puffy, too. How does your tummy feel? Does it hurt?'

'No.' Jennifer swallowed a bite of cereal. Suddenly her eyes grew huge. 'Excuse me!' she said, and flew into the bathroom, her mother close behind her.

'You poor little thing,' Mrs Tarkinton said, watching her miserable daughter lose her breakfast. 'If I didn't know better, I'd think you were pregnant.'

Jennifer stood up and stared at her mother. 'Oh, no,' she wailed, 'I'll bet I am!'

'That certainly puts a different complexion on things, doesn't it?' her father said that evening, a quick pregnancy test having confirmed Jennifer's suspicion.

'Yes, but I'm not sure just how,' Jennifer replied. 'I want the baby, of course, but I want it to have a father. Clay would be so happy about it. He's such a wonderful father to Pam.' Tears trickled down her cheeks. 'I wish he'd at least write to me. I'd write and tell him, but maybe he doesn't want to hear from me any more. Maybe he'd only think I was trying to use it to get him back!' She burst into racking sobs. 'I wish I'd never left him!' she choked out between gasps for air.

Then she buried her face in the sofa pillow while her mother patted her back soothingly and said, 'There, there.' She did not see the meaningful looks and the little nod of understanding that her parents exchanged above her head.

The next morning Jennifer's mother bundled her off to the doctor. 'To make sure everything's going along all right,' she said cheerily. 'I want my first grandchild to be perfect.' She frowned. 'I do wish you weren't going to be so far away.' Then she smiled again. 'I guess I'll just have to get used to flying out to see my little cowboy or cowgirl, won't I?'

'Mother,' Jennifer pointed out, 'it might be staying right here in Chicago.' She caught a suspicious twinkle in her mother's eyes. 'Mother,' she said severely, 'you haven't been meddling, have you?'

'Certainly not,' Mrs Tarkinton replied, looking hurt. 'I just have a feeling, that's all.'

'The only feeling I have is icky,' Jennifer said morosely. She had lain awake most of the night, thinking of Clay, remembering that night in the cabin and the overwhelming love that they had shared.

Several times she had reached for her telephone to call him, but each time had drawn back her trembling hand. He hadn't called her. Maybe he didn't want to hear from her. If only she knew for certain that he still loved her. She wouldn't blame him if he didn't.

That afternoon, Mrs Tarkinton dragged the reluctant Jennifer to the Art Institute to see a new exhibit.

'Perk up,' she told Jennifer firmly. 'The doctor says you're fine. Your father's meeting us downtown for dinner, too, and he's taking the day off tomorrow. We may have some . . . some other plans for then, too.'

'You're killing me with kindness,' Jennifer groaned. Nevertheless, she tried to be more lively, and when she complained that she looked too drab for a gala dinner her mother whisked her into a shop for a new dress, and then to her favourite beauty salon for a new hairdo and a facial.

'Now you look positively glamorous,' her mother said. 'How do you feel?'

'Better,' Jennifer admitted. The short, brushed-back hairstyle accented her elegant cheekbones, and the expert beautician's use of make-up made her look healthy and glowing.

'See that you do yourself like that in the morning,' her mother instructed, handing her the package of cosmetics she had bought to duplicate the beautician's magic. 'I'm tired of seeing you droop around the house, all pale and wan-looking. You'll feel better, too.'

'I'll do the best I can,' Jennifer promised. It was the least she could do to repay her mother for taking the shock so beautifully in stride.

She put on the make-up, as promised, before breakfast the next morning, but could find nothing to put on that was really comfortable around her slightly expanded waistline, so she settled for an old pair of trousers and a baggy shirt.

'Your face looks perfect,' her mother said brightly, as soon as she saw her, 'but those clothes just won't do. Come with me. I've got three pairs of trousers with stretchy waists that I bought before I lost some weight.' She soon had Jennifer dressed in bright, multicoloured striped trousers and a turquoise top. 'There,' she said, standing back to admire her daughter. 'I think you look good enough for anyone.'

Jennifer frowned suspiciously. 'Who is this anyone? Anyone I know?'

'Oh, I just meant . . . anyone who might happen along,' Mrs Tarkinton said with a vague smile.

'You're not a very good liar, Mother,' Jennifer said accusingly. 'I want to know what's going on. Something funny is, and I know it!'

'There's nothing funny going on, is there, dear?' Mrs Tarkinton said to her husband as they returned to the breakfast table.

'Not that I know of,' he replied, without looking up from his paper. 'Of course, there's a lot of funny business going on in the Middle East, as usual.'

Jennifer sighed resignedly and sat down. 'I guess I'm not going to get any straight answers from you two, am I?' she said. 'But I don't think it's very nice for you to keep whatever it is from me,' she added. Inside, a little flicker of excitement was building, in spite of her efforts to squelch it. The flicker revolved around one word. Clay.

After breakfast, her father looked at his watch. 'I'd better be off,' he said, getting up and giving both Jennifer and her mother a quick kiss. 'I've got an appointment in about an hour, but I'll be back by eleven.'

'We'll be looking for you,' Mrs Tarkinton said. 'Hurry back.'

'I thought he was taking the day off,' Jennifer said when he had gone.

'Oh, he is,' her mother replied. 'His appointment isn't business.' She smiled mysteriously at Jennifer and then quickly started to load the dishwasher. 'Darn!' she said, as a dish slipped from her fingers and shattered on the floor. She frowned. 'Jennifer, why don't you go and watch TV or something? It makes me nervous, the way you're staring at me.'

'All right,' Jennifer agreed with a wry little smile. 'But I don't think I'm what's making you nervous.'

Jennifer plopped down on the sofa and turned on the television. 'Ugh. Soap operas and game shows,' she said, and turned it off again. She picked up an old newspaper and began doing the crossword puzzle, but found that she could not even think of a four-letter word that meant slave. She went outside and looked at the neatly tended little yard. In the back, the huge oak tree with the steps nailed to its trunk where she had had her tree-house was still as lush and majestic as ever. 'I wonder if Clay ever had a tree-house?' she mused aloud, looking up into its branches. Maybe a boy with his own pony to ride across the immense expanse of the Bar-C Ranch didn't need such places to dream. She remembered dreaming dreams of riding like the wind, when the only wind in her hair had come through the branches of the tree. Then she had taken that ridiculous fall from the pony at the fair. She had never admitted that she had been trying to dismount and get back on while the pony had been moving, like someone she had seen in the films. Everyone had thought she was just clumsy, and her pride had been too badly wounded, along with her arm, for her to confess her deed.

'Jennifer? Oh, there you are.' Mrs Tarkinton appeared at the back door. 'I thought you'd wandered off. It's almost eleven.'

'Does that mean I'm supposed to come in, Mommy?' Jennifer teased, going to the door.

'Well, no, but I thought . . . maybe your father would have something for you when he got back.' Mrs Tarkinton smiled nervously.

Jennifer's heart did a little flip-flop. Was her hope that she scarcely dared hope, her dream that she was afraid to dream, to come true? Was Clay coming to see her? She followed her mother into the cosy living-room and sat down again with her puzzle, trying not to think of anything but the words on the page. She filled in several blanks, then flung the paper down.

'Mother, tell me the truth,' she demanded. 'Is Clay coming?'

Her mother looked at Jennifer, then out of the window, then at her watch. 'Well, I . . . uh . . .' she stammered, then jumped to her feet and peered out of the front window. 'Oh, good,' she said with a tremendous sigh of relief. 'Here comes your father now.' She turned and pushed Jennifer, who had stood up and started towards her, back to the sofa. 'You sit down and stay right there,' she said firmly. 'And don't peep.' With that she hurried to open the door.

Jennifer sat, not knowing whether to laugh or cry at her mother's excitement. Whatever was coming certainly had her almost flying apart from trying to keep the secret. She stood up again and waited, dutifully keeping her eyes averted from the large window, which looked out over the street and driveway. She heard the sound of three of the car's four doors opening and closing, then multiple footsteps on the path. Her mother stepped back, holding the door open. Her father came through the doorway, smiling broadly.

'I got more than I bargained for, Jennifer,' he said. 'I thought I'd be bringing you one friend, and I've brought three instead.' He stood aside, and Clay stepped into the room.

'Hello, Jenny, love,' he said, his smile so wide and welcoming that Jennifer flew into his waiting arms without a word. He folded his arms about her and swung her around and around. 'Oh, Jenny, how wonderful you look! How I do love you,' he said, at last lowering her to her feet again.

'Oh, Clay, I'm s-so happy,' Jennifer gasped through tears of joy. She crushed him to her, lost in the magic of his passionate embrace, floating towards heaven as Clay's mouth found hers and devoured her as if he could never get enough. Someone nearby cleared his throat loudly and Clay at last raised his head. 'Oh, yeah, I almost forgot,' he said, grinning over at Forrest. 'Say hello to the future Mrs Clayton Cooper.'

'Charmed, I'm sure,' Forrest said, his eyes twinkling as he bent to kiss Jennifer's cheek. 'I think you've already met my wife.' He pulled Tanya forwards from behind his back.

'Tanya!' Jennifer let go of Clay and flung her arms around the smaller woman. 'What a wonderful surprise!' She looked from Forrest to Clay. 'I don't understand. What's going on here?'

'Let's all sit down,' Mrs Tarkinton urged. 'I want to hear all about it, too. Jennifer's told us everything up until the time that she left.'

When everyone was seated, Jennifer snuggled

against Clay's shoulder, he began.

'Well, after Jenny left, I tried to talk to Matt, thinking that he had only refused to see me because he was temporarily upset. Much to my chagrin, he meant exactly what he'd said. In fact, he sent word that either Forrey and I got our act together, or he'd not only cut us both out of his will, but he'd send us off somewhere where we could grow turnips for a living for all he cared.'

Jennifer giggled. 'That sounds like Matt.'

'It sure does,' Clay agreed, hugging her against him. 'Anyway, after that Forrey and I had a fairly calm talk, and he finally convinced me that he was not the culprit that Barkley claimed. We decided to look into Jenny's suggestion that McDonald was behind the scheme instead. It suddenly occurred to both of us that we should go to the auction house and look at the duplicate sale tickets, something I should have thought of when you first discovered the shortage.' Clay looked down at Jennifer and made a wry face. 'Anyway, it turned out that Barkley's story was a complete fabrication. There were no missing cattle, only missing money. We got the auction house to look up the cancelled cheques, and discovered that they'd been cleared through a bank in the Cayman Islands. Then a smaller amount was put into the Bar-C account. We had a talk with Barkley, then, and he admitted the whole thing. The story was one that McDonald had invented to put us off the track, thinking that I'd be only too willing to believe that Forrey did it.' Clay grimaced and shook his head. 'I still can't believe I was so willing to let my worst side take over and almost lose everything that I cared for . . .' He gave Forrest a wink. 'And that includes my brother.'

Forrest smiled, a much more relaxed and happy

smile, Jennifer thought, than she had seen before. 'Clay
brought us along today because he didn't think Jennifer
would believe that we've declared a permanent truce
unless she saw it with her own eyes,' he said.

'I'm not sure I would have,' Jennifer agreed, 'but
that's an awfully long trip just to make a point.'

'Actually,' Tanya said, smiling her shy, sweet smile,
'we're here in Chicago for another reason. I'm going to
see a specialist about my problem in carrying a child.
We have hopes that we'll soon be able to have one.'

'How wonderful,' Jennifer said, feeling a little bubble
of excitement at the knowledge that she could soon tell
Clay her happy news, and it would truly be happy.

Clay chuckled. 'Another set of Matt's orders, once
he was speaking to us again, was for Forrey to get back
together with Tanya, me to come after Jenny and see
that she didn't send me off without her, and then for
someone to produce a grandchild as soon as possible.
He vows he's going to live to see at least one.'

'He sounds like quite a formidable man,' Jennifer's
father commented. 'Does he always try to arrange
everyone's lives for them like that?'

'He certainly does,' Jennifer said. 'The first time I
met him he practically ordered me to marry Clay. But
somehow, I didn't mind the idea at all, even then.' She
smiled up at Clay, who kissed the tip of her nose and
laughed.

'I'd already thought of it,' he said. He looked at
Forrest again. 'Matt did learn something, though, about
ordering lives around. At first he was worried that
Forrey might have really been involved in stealing some
of our cattle, and he said later that it made him wonder,
for the first time, if he had both driven Forrey to crime
and ruined his marriage by making him stay on the

ranch. After Forrey and I had settled our differences, Matt apologised and told him that he was free to do whatever he wanted.'

'Are you going to become a jazz musician now?' Jennifer asked.

Forrest shook his head. 'I might play a little in some of the local night spots, but I'm going to stay on the ranch. Dad still needs us, and it's the place I want to bring up a family.'

'You should have seen him out there during the round-up,' Clay said with a grin. 'Best cowhand I had.'

'There's one thing I still don't understand,' Jennifer said, frowning. 'What did poor Barkley get out of McDonald's scam? As far as I can see, he's still as poor as ever.'

'Not really,' Clay said. 'He got twenty thousand dollars from McDonald for playing the fall guy and trying to cover for him. Barkley used the money to buy a nice mobile home for his parents, who lived in a miserable old shack some place near Billings. He cried and was nearly frantic when we uncovered the whole story on McDonald, because he was sure McDonald would tell on him and he'd have to sell the mobile home.'

'Oh, the poor man,' Mrs Tarkinton said sympathetically. 'Will he have to go to jail?'

Clay shook his head. 'He's no criminal, and I think we can get him off with probation and keep him on at the Bar-C. He would never have chased Jenny if he hadn't been so terrified about his parents losing their first nice home. He cried about that, too, and swore if anything had happened to that nice Ms Tarkinton he would have died himself. I had trouble forgiving him for that.' Clay looked down at Jenny and smiled. 'Can you forgive him?'

'I guess so,' she said, 'since I wasn't really hurt. It was pretty exciting. Something to tell the children about.' She looked across at her mother and saw a flash of laughter in her eyes.

The look that passed between mother and daughter did not escape Clay's quick eye. He looked speculatively at Jennifer, but said nothing. Jennifer's father stood up suddenly.

'I hate to end this nice get-together, but I believe Tanya has an appointment downtown in a little over an hour. We'd better be on our way.'

'I'm coming too,' Mrs Tarkinton said. 'I think Jennifer and Clay have a lot to talk about. Tom and I will stay downtown tonight and take in a show.'

When everyone had left, Clay turned to Jennifer and put his hands on her shoulders, his face very serious, but his eyes flashing with mischief.

'All right, Jenny, my girl, out with it,' he said, trying to sound gruff. 'You're hiding something from me, aren't you?'

Jennifer tried to look wide-eyed and innocent. 'Why, Clay, whatever makes you say that?' she said, biting her lip to keep from bursting into happy laughter.

'Because when your father called he told me to get out here as fast as possible. That you needed to see me right away. I don't think he meant because you got your hair cut. I like it.'

'I'm so glad, because if you hadn't . . .' Jennifer could hold it in no longer. She flung her arms around Clay. 'We're going to have a baby,' she said.

The most beautiful smile Jennifer had ever seen spread slowly across Clay's face. 'Oh, Jenny,' he said softly. 'How wonderful.'

'Isn't it?' she agreed, her eyes misty with joy. 'I didn't want to say anything in front of Forrest and Tanya, because they've had such trouble and it's apparently so easy for us. The doctor says everything's fine.'

Wordlessly, Clay gathered Jennifer into his arms and carried her to the sofa. He sat down and cradled her in his arms. 'I don't know why,' he said, nibbling tenderly at her lips, 'but suddenly you seem much more fragile. I'll have to take very good care of you.'

'I'm not fragile at all,' Jennifer said, kissing him back. 'But I don't mind having you fuss over me. It's been a long time since I was sick and you sat by my bed and fed me like a baby.' She frowned and cocked her head to one side. 'As a matter of fact, I have a bone to pick with you, Clayton Cooper. Why didn't you write or call for so long? I've been so miserable I thought I'd die, and I was afraid to call you for fear you'd stopped loving me.'

'That will never happen, Jenny,' Clay said seriously. 'Never.' He smiled whimsically. 'I was miserable, too, and I had plenty of help. Pam wouldn't talk to me, Nell put the food away as soon as dinner was over and wouldn't feed me if I was late, and Clarence came right out and told me I was a fool. It wasn't until everyone knew I was working towards getting you back that things settled down a little.' He held Jennifer close and sighed deeply. 'I was so lonely. I wanted to call so many times, but it took Forrey and me a while to set things right between us, and I couldn't very well ask you to come back, tell you everything was fine, and then have it all fall apart again. I couldn't bear to hurt you like that.'

'That's the way my parents felt, too,' Jennifer said. She told Clay of their almost miraculous change. 'I'm so happy for them,' she concluded. 'And for you and Forrest and Tanya.'

'And Matt,' Clay added. 'All of his fondest wishes are going to come true, if he can only hold out for a while longer.' He grinned. 'And I think he's stubborn enough to do it.'

'I think so too,' Jennifer agreed. She smiled as Clay stifled a yawn. 'Tired?'

Clay nodded. 'I didn't sleep a wink last night, wondering what you needed to see me about. We already had the plane tickets and were going to surprise you, because I was too cowardly to call ahead of time and find out you had a new boyfriend or something. Then, when your father called . . .' He held Jennifer close. 'I wondered if you might be pregnant, but it seemed too good to be true, so I thought of all the terrible things that might have happened instead.'

'Maybe you'd like to take a little nap,' Jennifer suggested.

A bright gleam lighted Clay's eyes. 'With you?'

Jennifer smiled. 'You bet, with me. I'm not letting you out of my sight again for a long, long time. Come on, I'll lead you to my room.'

'Just give me directions,' Clay said, standing up with Jennifer in his arms. 'We'll close the door and pretend we're back in the cabin again. That night was even more special than we dreamed, wasn't it?'

'It certainly was.' Jennifer pointed the way to her bedroom, then closed the door and pulled down the shades. Moments later, she and Clay were nestled against each other, their bare bodies melting together blissfully. 'Here we are,' she whispered, her heart beating faster and faster as Clay's hands stroked her lovingly, 'in a cowboys' cabin in the mountains. I've just promised to marry my own real cowboy. Outside, the thunder is crashing and the lightning flashing, but inside——'

'But inside,' Clay said softly, 'we're finding heaven. I think we're about to find it again, and this time we'll never let it go.'

2 NEW TITLES FOR JUNE 1990

PASSAGES by Debbi Bedford
Shannon Eberle's dreams had catapulted her to the height of fame and fortune in New York City. But when the lights went out on Broadway, she found herself longing for home and the people she'd left behind. So Shannon returned to Wyoming, where she met Peter Barrett, a strong and gentle man who taught her to dream anew...
£2.99

ALL MY TOMORROWS by Karen Young
Carly Sullivan was a woman who trusted her heart. For her it was easy to see the solution to the problems Jess Brannigan was having with his estranged son. For Jess, seeing what a little tender loving care could achieve was a revelation. An even greater surprise was the difference Carly made in his own life!
£2.99

W●RLDWIDE

Available from Boots, Martins, John Menzies, W.H. Smith, Woolworths and other paperback stockists.

TWO COMPELLING READS FOR MAY 1990

TESS   *Katherine Burton*   £2.99

In the third book of this sensational quartet of sisters, the bestselling author of *Sweet Summer Heat* creates Tess. Tormented by the guilt of her broken marriage and afraid to risk the pain again, Tess is torn by desire. But was Seth Taylor the right choice in helping her to get over the pain of the past?

SPRING THUNDER   *Sandra James*   £2.99

After a traumatic divorce and the unfamiliar demands of a new born son, Jessica is determined to start a new life running a garden centre. Tough, reliable Brody was hired to help, but behind the facade of job hunting is hidden the fact that he was being paid to destroy Jessica…whatever the cost.

W❂RLDWIDE

DREAM SONG TITLES COMPETITION
HOW TO ENTER

Listed below are 5 incomplete song titles. To enter simply choose the missing word from the selection of words listed and write it on the dotted line provided to complete each song title.

A. . . . . .DREAMS   LOVER

B.   DAY DREAM . . . .   ELECTRIC

C.   DREAM . . . .   CHRISTMAS

D.   . . . . UPON A DREAM   BELIEVER

E.   I'M DREAMING OF A WHITE . . . .   ONCE

When you have completed each of the song titles, fill in the box below, placing the songs in an order ranging from the one you think is the most romantic, through to the one you think is the least romantic.

Use the letter corresponding to the song titles when filling in the five boxes. For example: If you think C. is the most romantic song, place the letter C. in the 1st box.

	1st	2nd	3rd	4th	5th
LETTER OF CHOSEN SONG					

MRS/MISS/MR . . . .

ADDRESS . . . .

. . . .

POSTCODE . . . . COUNTRY . . . .

CLOSING DATE: 31st DECEMBER, 1990
PLEASE SEND YOUR COMPLETED ENTRY TO EITHER:
Dream Book Offer, Eton House, 18-24 Paradise Road, Richmond, Surrey, ENGLAND TW9 1SR.

OR (Readers in Southern Africa)
Dream Book Offer, IBS Pty Ltd., Private Bag X3010, Randburg 2125, SOUTH AFRICA.

- - - - ✂ -